SWEET
DECEIT

SWEET COUNTY SECRETS SERIES
BOOK ONE

SALLY JO PITTS

ELK LAKE PUBLISHING INC.®

PUBLISHING THE POSITIVE
Plymouth, Massachusetts

A Christian Company
ElkLakePublishingInc.com

COPYRIGHT NOTICE

Cover and Interior Design: Derinda Babcock, Deb Haggerty
Editor(s): Cristel Phelps, Deb Haggerty

PUBLISHED BY: Elk Lake Publishing, Inc., 35 Dogwood Drive, Plymouth, MA 02360, 2024

Library Cataloging Data
Names: Pitts, Sally Jo (Sally Jo Pitts)
Sweet Deceit / Sally Jo Pitts
p. 23cm × 15cm (9in × 6 in.)
ISBN-13: 9798891341388 (paperback) | 9798891341395 (trade paperback) | 9798891341401 (e-book)
Key Words: Christian Mystery & Suspense Romance; Christian Mystery Books; Christian Mystery Romance Books; Small Town Police Romance; Clean and Wholesome Romance; Cozy Mystery; Mystery/Suspense Romance
Library of Congress Control Number: 2024932482 Fiction

DEDICATION

In Memory of LaVelle—

Whose experiences when he was appointed sheriff in a small Florida county provided the inspiration for *Sweet Deceit*.

ACKNOWLEDGMENTS

A book takes many dedicated helpers to make it come together. I am so grateful to editors Deb Haggerty and Cristel Phelps of Elk Lake Publishing, Inc.

Marcia Lahti for content editing and suggestions, Kelly Pitts for proofreading, and the beta readers who contributed comments.

I especially acknowledge my husband, LaVelle, who has since gone to be with the Lord. He conferred with me on this project in its early stages, and plot ideas were sparked from his years in law enforcement.

Be not deceived; God is not mocked: for whatsoever a man soweth, that shall he also reap.

—Galatians 6:7

CHAPTER 1

Could things finally be looking up for Annie McAfee?

Driving from Tallahassee to Sugarville on Florida's I-10, Annie settled in behind a truck pulling a horse trailer to pace her speed while mulling over her job interview at the governor's office.

She had responded to all the questions for the public relations job with confidence. But had she answered too quickly? Or been too wordy? The interviewer had glanced at his watch twice. Her dad used to make the same furtive moves before announcing, "Annie, you're prattling."

Event ideas spun in her head. She wanted this job. She could do this job. But she also knew the game. A staff member quizzed a required number of applicants, and an insider, already earmarked, would be awarded the job.

She huffed a sigh. "Going through the process is still good experience."

Talking out loud ensured she had a listener. She might as well get used to one-sided conversations, rattling around by herself in the Victorian parsonage overlooking the Sugarville Community Church, where her father had recently become pastor. The plan was to housesit for her parents who were on a mission trip in Brazil for the summer while she waitressed and explored employment options.

The horse trailer slowed and moved into the same exit she needed. Flicking on her turn signal, she glanced into the rearview mirror. The same white truck that had followed her since Tallahassee turned on his blinker.

All three vehicles proceeded down the off ramp and turned right onto the two-lane road toward Sweet County. The scenario was hardly unusual, but an odd feeling she'd learned to pay attention to tugged at her senses. This exit offered no gas stations or other conveniences, just a country highway bordered by trees and fields for miles in either direction.

The truck behind her sped up and closed the space between them. Annie moved further to the right to allow the truck to pass. The grill of the truck loomed large until all she could see was the top of the hood. *Shoot.* Was he going to run into her? She tapped her accelerator and gained on the horse trailer.

The truck suddenly roared past, then slammed on brakes. She braked as he squeezed in between her and the horse trailer. Strange. There was a broken center line on the road for passing and there was no oncoming traffic. If he was in a rush, why hadn't he continued around the trailer?

The white truck braked again, slowing below 30mph. The terrain had changed into wooded pines with hills, making passing dangerous. Now she was stuck behind him. The horse trailer disappeared around a turn.

Creeping along, she stared at the red bumper sticker on the truck that said nothing, since only the bottom half remained. Was he playing a game? Having engine trouble? Looking for a side road?

At last, a broken line indicated safe passing. The driver of the truck stuck out his arm and motioned for her to pass. There was no traffic ahead.

Annie pulled into the oncoming lane, but when she came alongside the truck, he matched her speed. She accelerated but he inched closer to the center line.

Way too close.

She attempted to drop behind him, but he blocked her. Again, she sped up, but he matched her speed. The grill of the truck glared in the sunlight. *What was he doing?* He closed in with magnetic force. Her speed reached sixty. A sign ahead warned of a sharp turn.

Lord, this is Annie. E-mer-gen-cy!

The truck surged again, lining up with her passenger door. The driver wore a ball cap, mirrored sunglasses, and a smirk. He swerved, and steel met steel in a hard dull thud.

The car lurched.

"Are you crazy!" Annie screamed. With wheels squealing and the braking stench of burning rubber, her car careened from the road, tilting on two wheels. Struggling to gain control, the car slammed down on all fours.

The truck rammed her again from the rear, jolting her across weeds, rocks, and underbrush.

Focus. When in peril, suppress panic. Annie worked the brakes. The action whirled her around, impeding the forward trajectory. She finally ground to a halt perpendicular to the road.

A hazy dust cloud of dirt shrouded her vision. Gripping the steering wheel, she shuddered, and her heart hammered in her chest. The truck's engine revved, and its tires sprayed an arch of dirt and roared away.

"Thank you, Lord." The words, like globs of glue, stuck in her throat.

Pushing the gearshift into park, her trembling fingers fumbled for the key to shut off the engine. A billboard nearby proclaimed, YOU JUST ENTERED SWEET COUNTY, FLORIDA. Underneath, scrawled in red paint, were the added words—*at your own risk.*

"Amen, brother," Annie muttered and waved away the fine sand particles coating her nose and throat.

She unhooked her seatbelt. Climbing from the car, she clung to the door to steady her shaky legs.

Why did that man force her off the road? Was this some weird backwoods chicken game?

Her car had stopped against a small pine sapling that stood next to a drop off. She stepped closer, then shrank back at the dizzying sight. A steep gorge, at least thirty feet deep, marked by gullies and craggy bushes loomed over the edge.

Circling her car, her dress shoes took on sand as she inspected the damage. Her taillight was cracked, the rear fender dented, the front fender scratched. Another small pine tree was stuck beneath her bumper, but she couldn't get it to budge.

"Great." She patted her pine-sapped hands in the sandy soil to cover the sticky residue then ran her fingers over the crumpled indention on the car door.

Things were *not* looking up for Annie McAfee after all.

Rookie Florida Department of Law Enforcement agent Will Brice, the lone inhabitant inside the Sweet County Sheriff's Office, drummed impatient fingers on the front desk. By order of the governor, Sheriff Wayne Daly had been removed from office. Game and Fish Commission officer Ray Goutter was appointed as interim sheriff.

Because of Will's prior experience working in a sheriff's office, he'd been pulled from a FDLE team working on a high-profile murder case in south Florida to help the provisional sheriff for a few days. Twiddling his thumbs did not sit well with Will. So far, his mission had been to purchase notepads, pens, and toilet paper.

"Keep the receipt," Sheriff Goutter had said. "When Governor Renfroe told Sheriff Daly to vacate, Daly and his men left nothing behind."

On Will's return from the store, Goutter met him at the door and plunked a small key in his hand. "This key fits the former sheriff's top desk drawer. You handle the calls for a while. I've got business to tend to in Tallahassee."

One of the two phone lines beeped and lit up. Will answered.

"I need to talk to Sheriff Daly. Is he in?"

"Sorry, but he's been removed from office by the governor."

"Maybe that governor should be booted out instead of our sheriff."

He could sympathize with the citizen caller who didn't want an outsider in the sheriff's office. Even though Sheriff Daly had been involved in questionable activities, he seemed to have garnered loyalty.

In between answering calls, Will mapped out a crash course on sheriff's office administration. All he needed was Sheriff Goutter to present it to.

Will tapped his fingers on his outlined notes, then noticed movement in his peripheral vision. A grasshopper bounced along the floor and landed on the entry door. Will pushed out of the hard oak desk chair and opened the door to let the critter out. "You don't belong here, either."

A man in uniform stood at the open door. "I didn't expect door service."

"An officer with a friendly face deserves door service." Will held the door open for the man, who climbed the short flight of stairs and stepped onto the worn linoleum floor. Adjusting his gun belt, he thrust a beefy hand out to grab Will's. "I'm Sugarville Police Chief Jim Woodham."

"Will Brice, FDLE special agent, sent to assist Sheriff Goutter. How can I help you?"

"I came to ask that question. Is Sheriff Goutter here?"

"Gone to Tallahassee, but I expect him any time."

Woodham nodded, looked around, then peered into the private office of the sheriff. "Looks pretty well cleaned out."

"Yes, sir. I had to purchase a few supplies. You wouldn't have a spare radio operator, would you? I'm stuck if I get a call from someone needing assistance."

"My patrolmen work inside the city limits and can help out if they aren't tied up. But I hear you. The sheriff needs someone in this office he can rely on." The chief made a sucking sound drawing air through his teeth. "I have a part-time operator I use if somebody's sick or takes leave. I'll call her and see if she's free."

"Hearing the voice of someone local might help callers accept an outsider taking over the sheriff's office a bit better."

Chief Woodham held up his hands in resignation. "Sweet Countians may be resistant, but they're resilient. They'll warm up to you."

"Ray Goutter is the one they need to warm to. I'm just here long enough to help him with the transition."

The chief hung his thumbs on his gun belt. "Appreciate you comin'. Anything else I can help with?"

Will requested incident report forms.

The minute the chief left, the phone rang, and the caller asked to speak to Sheriff Daly. Will tried a different approach, leaving off the part about the governor removing the sheriff.

"He's no longer here."

"What do you mean, he's no longer here?"

"He was asked to step down for not carrying out his sworn duties. But I can offer help."

"Only way you can help me is to put Sheriff Daly on the phone." The caller's don't-tread-on-me attitude crackled in his ear before hanging up.

Will understood small county pride. Raised in rural, neighboring Hill County, he'd experienced the sense of anger and helplessness that comes when someone you care for is taken from you.

He traced the outline of SOS letters someone had carved into the top of the wood desk. Where was Sheriff Goutter?

CHAPTER 2

Her hands still shaky, Annie adjusted her visor against the sun's rays. Why would anyone try to harm her? She'd only been in town a short time, and few people knew her. Fifteen more minutes of passing farmland with young crops of corn and sugarcane and she'd be at the Sugarville police station.

She entered the city limits on Confection Street. Sugarville's founders had designed the city with a dessert book in one hand and a compass in the other. Roads running north and south were designated as streets, east and west were avenues. The police station stood on Pie Avenue directly behind Candy's Café where she waitressed.

Annie attempted to pull to the curb, but the pesky tree attached to her bumper presented scratchy resistance. She had to park at a lopsided angle. As she got out of the car, she whiffed a mix of turpentine and gasoline smells coming from her pitiful looking Ford Fiesta.

Inside the police station, a lone officer sat at the front desk talking into the phone cradled on his shoulder. He motioned for her to take a seat in one of the metal chairs lining the wall.

"Yes, sir. I'll see that the chief gets your invitation." He finished his call, turned to Annie, and his face brightened.

"You're the new waitress at Candy's. I almost didn't recognize you without your apron. What brings you here?"

"I suppose I do look different. I had a job interview in Tallahassee this morning, but on the way back I ran into trouble, or I should say trouble ran into me and—"

The phone buzzed with an incoming call.

The officer nodded toward the window. "The chief is just returning from the sheriff's office. He can take your complaint. Excuse me. This phone is keeping me busier than usual today."

"Looks like somebody is using their car to harvest pine trees," the chief said as he walked in the door.

Annie stood. "My car brought down the tree, but harvesting was not my intention."

"I wondered why I didn't see you at the café. Candy said you'd gone to Tallahassee. So, what's the story? Did you run after the tree or did the tree jump out at you?"

Annie's back stiffened at his little joke. "Some rogue in a white truck forced me off the road."

"Forced?" He tilted his head and frowned. "Come into my office, and I'll take a report on your allegation."

Allegation? Annie wasn't sure whether to interpret his facial expression as a look of concern or doubt. She trailed behind Chief Woodham. He walked with an uneven gait as if his shoes pinched his feet, just like his questioning words pinched her attitude.

She took a seat in front of his desk covered with various stacks of files, catalogs, brochures for ATVs and two Styrofoam cups. He retrieved a form from the shelf behind him, placed it on top of a folder, and prepared to write. "Your first name is Annie. I hear Candy call it out all the time. Last name?"

"McAfee. M-c-capital-A-f-e-e.

"McAfee. Isn't that the name of the new pastor at Sugarville Community?"

"Yes, sir. I'm house sitting for Mom and Dad while they're away on a mission trip."

"So, you're living in the old Fleming house." He peered at her over the top of his glasses. "Mighty brave."

Annie cocked a brow. "I've heard rumors about ghosts and the lion statues coming to life and prowling at night. Do you believe the stories?"

Furrows deepened in his forehead. A test of her fortitude? "An old house sitting on a hill attracts rumors and stories. Old man Fleming kept to himself, so naturally, a lot of mystery surrounds the place. After his nephew sold the house, some say the night noises became more frequent."

"I have no ghosts to report. Only a creaky old house that may have rats in the basement."

"Try a spring trap or poison."

"I'd rather try catch and release."

"Uh-huh." He looked at her as if she had two heads. "Now suppose you tell me about being run off the road."

Annie described the incident to the point of the driver motioning her to pass. "When I was alongside the truck, the driver sped up, crossed the line, and rammed into me. I barely escaped toppling into a deep ravine."

"Winchester Ravine?

"I don't know the name."

"At the county line?"

"Yes. I came to a stop near an entering Sweet County billboard."

He rubbed his chin and tapped the form with the end of his pen. "This happened outside my jurisdiction. You'll need to report the incident to the sheriff's office."

"Wasn't the sheriff just fired by the governor?"

"Yes. Ray Goutter is the appointed interim." Chief Woodham closed his ballpoint pen with a click.

"Is he equipped to handle an attempted murder?"

His condescending snort raked over her. "You're overstating this a bit, aren't you?"

"No, sir." Her jaw tightened at the insinuation. Why didn't he take her word at face value? She counted backwards from ten in her head.

He held up a hand. "You need to understand that attempted murder is a serious charge."

"I know. That's why I'm here."

Her remark brought up both his hands. "Okay. You can report what you think happened. I just came from the sheriff's office. Goutter isn't there, but a state agent who came to assist him is on duty. He's capable of taking your report."

"Rules are rules?"

"Afraid so." If he intended his smile to be sympathetic, it missed its mark.

She gathered her purse and stood to leave. He crumpled the report he no longer needed, tossed and popped it off the wall, making a perfect drop into the trash basket. She wasn't certain if his triumphant "yes" was for the ringed basket or getting rid of her.

The sheriff's office was on a side street on the opposite side of the courthouse square. The pine tree under her car made a swishing sound as it swept the street on the way to the Sweet County Sheriff's Office. She parked horizontal to the street to avoid taking up too much room from the obstruction sticking out of her bumper.

Inside the red brick building, a man with reddish close-cropped hair stood studying a map hung on the wall. He held the phone receiver to his ear, and when he glimpsed at her, he nodded and held up an index finger.

Suddenly aware of her appearance, Annie straightened her skirt and jacket and smoothed hair that probably looked frightful after her ordeal. There was little she could do about the layer of dust on her navy heels that had been nice and shiny for her job interview that morning. She approached the desk, which held a base radio, notepad, and phone.

"Old Water Tower Road. Yes, I'll hold." His eyes caught hers. He gave her an inquiring look and covered the mouthpiece. "Ma'am?"

"The police chief sent me over—"

"Bless him."

Bless him? Into the phone he said, "An ambulance is on the way? Good. I'll be headed that way too."

He hung up, grabbed the notepad off the desk, and motioned to a plastic bag on the floor. "There's another notepad and pen in there for taking calls. I'll be on the radio, assuming it works. You're in charge."

He turned and hurried out the door.

Annie stared after him. In charge? She did a 360. Had Candid Camera found Sugarville? But no TV guy came out laughing and telling her how funny she looked. She peered out the window into the parking lot and watched the sheriff's car departing.

Throwing up her hands, she plunked down on the hard wood chair behind the desk.

Will cranked the Sweet County patrol car and glanced at the gas gauge. The pointer remained on the E. He smacked the steering wheel. "Great. No sheriff and no gas."

Will had noticed a gas station a block away when he arrived in town. He drove to the station, thankful the car made it, and pulled beside one of the two pumps.

In a car stall, a man raised his head from under the hood of an old Mercury sedan. Wiping his hands on an already greasy red cloth, he approached the patrol car. Brown curls, anchored by a backward ball cap, fringed his forehead. 'Rex' embroidered on the pocket of his coveralls gave him a name, and he had a lazy eye that made it hard to discern which of his eyes to focus on.

"You the new sheriff?"

"Assistant. I'm helping out. Does the sheriff's office have an account here?"

"Sheriff Daly has an account." One of the man's eyes examined him. "Now that you people are in, I don't know."

"I'm answering a hit-and-run call. I'm out of gas. I'll pay for it if you want, and the county can reimburse me." Will reached into his back pocket and pulled out his wallet.

Rex waved him off. "No need. I suppose I can take a chance on you." He unscrewed the gas cap, lifted the pump handle, and started pumping the gas.

Will got out of the car. "I didn't know there were gas stations left where the gas is pumped for the customers."

Rex lifted his chin and sniffed. "In Sweet County, we hold to the old traditions."

Will squeegeed the windshield.

"Hit-and-run, you say?" Rex asked.

"Mr. Jenkins on Old Water Tower Road witnessed an SUV running into a car and leaving the scene."

"I worked on Mr. Jenkins's truck last month. It was runnin' hot. Heater hose shot." The pump clicked off. Rex returned the handle to its holder. "Straight shooter, Mr. Jenkins is."

Will focused on Rex's right eye. "Good. That makes my fact-gathering a lot easier. What's the best way to go to Old Water Tower Road from here?"

Rex scratched his head. "Well, sir, you could go down County Road 306, but I wouldn't recommend it. Road work would slow you down. They're repairing a bridge, and it's about time. The guard rail has been down for months with only safety cones to warn drivers. Probably best to turn right on Sweet Street, go down to Sugar Avenue, turn left. Go about half a mile till you come to the old Fleming house. Made it into a parsonage, but you couldn't get me to live there. House sits up on a hill and has big ol' lion statues sitting by the drive. Can't miss it. Turn right there. Go maybe two miles, give 'er take, past the blueberry farm and turn left. Then, the first left is Old Water Tower Road. If you see the house with the blue tin roof, you've gone too far. It's easy to miss that turn. The Jenkins farm is down maybe a quarter mile on the right."

"Is there a sign at the blueberry farm?"

"Can't say for sure." He scratched his head. "Maybe. Everybody just knows where it's at."

Will shook his head. "Not everybody."

"It's got a wooden fence mostly covered with vines. You best learn these landmarks if you're gonna be sheriff."

"Ray Goutter is your interim sheriff. I'm only here temporarily. Thanks for the gas and directions."

"I wish you luck. Tell Mr. Jenkins I said hello."

"I'll do that."

Will followed a mental map of Rex's narrative. Right on Sweet, left on Sugar, right at lions, left at blueberry farm. Will slowed and searched for the vine-covered fence. It had been some time since he'd received directions using landmarks. On patrol in the Jacksonville area, travel instructions were issued using compass point directions, highway numbers, and street names.

The sight of a school bus, dropping preschool age youngsters at a country bus shelter, made his stomach roll. Twenty springtimes had passed since he disembarked at a similar bus stop as a nine-year-old and walked the quarter of a mile to the family farm. That day had changed his life. The day his mother died. The ache, though less intense, remained.

Sun spotlighted a blue tin roof on the farmhouse just ahead. Lengthy country directions encompassed not only how to get somewhere but the pitfalls. Will made a three-point turn and located the easy to miss road.

At the accident site, the ambulance had arrived and both victims were being tended. A man wearing a straw hat with a stained sweat band, overalls, and a plaid shirt walked toward him.

"Howdy. You the new sheriff?"

"No, sir." Will stepped out of the patrol car and shook the man's calloused hand. "Will Brice. I'm here to help acquaint the governor's appointee with the job, but he had business in Tallahassee." Will nodded toward the ambulance. "I appreciate you getting help here. I won't interfere with their work. How are the accident victims?"

"Sam and Helen Thornton are pretty shook up. A new-looking silver or gray SUV hit the Thornton's Oldsmobile and backed up. I figured the driver would pull over, but he roared off in that direction." Mr. Jenkins pointed north. "Probably a kid, hopped up on something, out joy riding. A lot 'a good us being a dry county does. Law-abiding citizens can't get a drink, but ask a teen, and I guarantee he knows how to get whiskey and a whole lot more."

"License number?"

"Never saw the tag. I was more concerned about the Thorntons. Helen's head must have hit the dash. Sam is hurt worse." Jenkins kicked at a rock in the dirt drive. "Teenagers think they're invincible and don't consider consequences. The Thorntons' car is probably totaled. The kid may be hurt."

"If you don't mind waiting, I need to call the station, then take your statement."

Will returned to his car. He unclipped the mic on the police radio and depressed the call button.

"Brice to Sweet County."

Nothing.

"Brice to Sweet County, you read?"

Static crackled, then nothing.

"Sweet County, I can't hear you, but if you hear me, call the FHP to send an officer to Old Water Tower Road about a quarter mile north of County Road 2034."

He waited. Finally, a faint voice answered.

"Got it. I'll call."

"10-4." He shook his head and wondered if they used the same 10 codes in Sweet County as he was accustomed to. He made a mental note to write the FHP frequency information for Goutter.

Will finished jotting down details furnished by Mr. Jenkins and delivered the hello message from Rex at the gas station. The ambulance pulled away as an FHP officer arrived in a black and gold cruiser. "Aaron Newsome," he said in greeting. "What's the story here?"

Mr. Jenkins shared what he'd observed, and Will explained his temporary status and the need for the Highway Patrol to take the lead on the hit-and-run.

"The person who caused this wreck will likely go out of area to repair his vehicle, but it would be helpful if you could notify auto body shops in Sweet County to be on the lookout for the damaged car," Newsome said. "I'll do the same in the Tallahassee area."

Thankful to have FHP take over, Will cued the mic. "Brice, Sweet County, 10-98 accident scene. 10-51."

No response.

Ten minutes later, he pulled into the sheriff's office, noting the red Ford Fiesta parked next to the road with a tree branch sticking out. He gathered his pad and pen and went inside. "Any word from Sheriff Goutter?"

"Uh ... no, but—"

Will sighed and sank heavily into the chair in front of the reception desk. "Many calls come in?"

"A few, but—"

"I need you to look up all the listings for auto shops and health care facilities in Sweet County." Will flipped open his notepad and scribbled a reminder to himself to check with Rex about anyone who did auto body work and might not be listed in the phone book.

"I can, but—" The operator slapped her hands on the desk. "Don't you want to know why I'm here?"

Will startled at the urgency in her voice. Indignation flashed in her brown eyes, and she folded her arms across her middle. How had he drawn her ire? "I know you're here to answer the phone, but maybe not to look up numbers?"

"You think I was sent to work here?"

"Weren't you?"

"No." She pushed the notepad in front of her toward him. "I'm here to file a complaint."

CHAPTER 3

By the expression on the agent's face, Annie could tell she had truly taken him off guard. A hint of red flushed his neck, coloring his rugged good looks.

"But you said the police chief sent you over."

"He did," she said with a hand shrug. "To file a complaint."

"I'm sorry. I thought the chief had sent a radio operator to help answer calls."

Annie offered a small smile. "I figured that out when you left."

"And you even tried to answer the radio."

Annie smirked. "I tried."

He stood, combing his fingers through his hair. "You must think me—"

She held up her hand, "—over-extended with no help. I'm Annie, by the way." She offered her hand. "Annie McAfee."

He grasped her hand. "Will Brice. I appreciate your understanding. I am so sorry to have held you up. Do you have time to file your complaint now?"

"I suppose." She glanced at the clock. "It's 12:45. I have to be at work at three."

He sat back down, clicked his pen, and flipped to a new page in his notebook. All business.

"Address?"

"The parsonage, 815 Sugar Avenue. I'm house-sitting for my parents." She gave him her place of work and phone numbers.

"Your complaint?"

"Someone tried to kill me."

He quit writing, looked up, and held her gaze. Was he waiting for her to say just kidding? She matched his stare, unflinching. He returned to his paper. "Tell me the particulars. Who, what, when, where, and why."

"The what, when, and where are that I was deliberately forced off the road by somebody in a white pickup at the county line this morning around ten o'clock. The who and why is what I'm hoping you can find out."

"Did you see the tag number?"

"No. Well, yes, I saw the tag, but I had no reason to commit it to memory. I didn't realize the guy was going to try to do me in."

"Extended cab?"

"Uh ... not sure."

"Make?"

Annie pressed her brows together. Self-incrimination judged her. She made a horrible witness. Agent Brice looked up from his notepad.

"I'm not sure ... I'm sorry. I guess I'm not giving you much to go on, but the truck had a red bumper sticker."

"What was on the bumper sticker?"

Annie wrinkled her nose. "Nothing. The top half of the sticker was missing. What I remember most were the driver's mirror glasses and malicious grin. He looked like an evil alien."

Agent Brice tapped his pen on the pad. "Were there other vehicles around?"

"A truck with a horse trailer had been ahead of us but had gone out of view when this happened."

"Why do you think he purposely ran you off the road?"

"I don't know. He had motioned for me to go around him. When I did, he swerved and hit me."

"Could you have been in his blind spot, and he pulled out to pass the horse trailer?"

"I ... I don't know ... no... no, he motioned for me to pass."

"Maybe he was motioning to the trailer that he was passing."

"Wait. Are you making excuses for this guy?"

"No. I'm trying to understand what happened."

"The guy looked at me with a horrid grin when he struck me. I barely escaped plunging down a cliff."

"What reason would anyone have to try and harm you?"

"None ... that I know of."

He scrutinized her a moment, and she held eye contact. Was he trying to decide if she was delusional? He snapped his ballpoint pen closed. "I know you have to go to work. Is that your car out front with the pine tree underneath?"

She nodded.

"If I can get someone to handle the phone, I'd like you to show me the place where the incident occurred. I'll take photos of the accident site and the damage to your car. Your insurance will require that information."

"I hadn't thought about insurance."

He said nothing, but his expression spoke of uncertainty, like Chief Woodham's. Did he suspect her claim was a ruse to collect insurance?

Within thirty minutes of Agent Brice contacting Chief Woodham, Winnie Melrose arrived with incident forms, a phone message book, and ready to handle calls.

Outside, Will opened the passenger door of the patrol car for Annie. "You don't need to open my door. I'm already taking up a lot of your time."

"Helping is my job until Sheriff Goutter returns."

He slid into the driver's seat. "Call me Will. Is it all right to call you Annie?"

"Of course."

As he was backing out, the rear tire dropped into a pothole, making the rear bumper scrape against the pavement. "I need to add having the city repair that hole on my list of recommendations for Goutter. Point me in the right direction."

"The incident happened at the county line just off the I-10 exit."

"Easy enough. I came into town from I-10."

"Do you mind my asking how you were selected to assist the appointed sheriff?"

He shrugged. "Low man on the totem pole. I had just achieved state investigator status, but being a newcomer with sheriff's office experience landed me here. Wrong place, wrong time."

He glanced at her with a hint of a smile. She could relate. Annie was queen of the wrong place and time. Ask her mom and dad. She returned the slight smile and would have said more, but the Sweet County billboard came into view. "The guy swerved and ran me off the road on the curve in front of that billboard."

Will stopped short of the sign. "I want to take an overall picture of the roadside, then scout for evidence."

He pulled out his camera and began taking photos. His skill at adjusting lenses and angles interested her.

"Where did you go off the road?"

"Further up, around the curve."

They walked ahead until she saw the indentions her tires had left. "There. You can see my tracks in the sand. I ground to a halt against that little pine and freaked when I saw how close I was to sailing into nothingness. According to Chief Woodham, this big hole is known as Winchester Ravine."

Will peered into the yawning chasm. "That is quite a drop." He took several more photos.

Annie pointed to the billboard. "I'd like to add a few exclamation points to the 'at your own risk' somebody painted on the entering Sweet County sign."

Will didn't comment. He walked past the place she'd run off the road and took a shot of the approach. Then zeroed in on the skid marks. He squatted down and took a closeup of something that glinted in the sun. "Did you lose trim off your car?"

"No."

"This piece of chrome may have come from the truck when he sideswiped you."

"So, you believe me?"

"I never disbelieved you. There is intent and fault that evidence alone won't substantiate. But your perception is yours."

"I'm sorry to be defensive, but this incident should be taken seriously. I'm concerned Chief Woodham might think I'm mistaken about the accident being deliberate."

"Understandable." He continued to examine the road. "We constantly deal with people's opinions, but we are also fact gatherers."

Was he giving her double talk? Did he believe her along with being skeptical? She had a lifetime of experience with skeptics, although admittedly, she'd given reason for skepticism. She had a way of embellishing situations, but those days were behind her, and this episode was neither in her imagination nor an exaggeration.

"Photos and this report will back your claim for insurance and could help find the culprit. However, the suspect is likely having his vehicle fixed to be rid of the evidence."

"The hit-and-run you worked on Old Water Tower Road. Could it be the same person?"

"No. The accident on Old Water Tower Road involved a silver or gray SUV. Leave the metal strip where it is and wait here. I need to get my evidence gathering supplies, and I'll move the car closer."

Will walked away, disappearing around the curve. Relief touched Annie's spirit. Will seemed to take her seriously.

Annie stooped down, studying the chrome trim closely, careful not to move or touch it. A motor idled somewhere nearby. She stood and walked slowly up the road away from the curve, searching carefully for any other evidence.

The roar of an engine surged behind her.

Annie's heart jackknifed.

The metal grill of a truck bore down on her with the intensity of a branding iron ready to singe flesh. A scream lodged in her throat.

The truck veered toward her.

Adrenaline pulsed as Annie dove to the side of the road. Dirt and debris gouged into her skin.

The vehicle thundered past, barely missing her feet and sending an extra layer of gritty sand and dust on top of her. Tires screeching, the truck fishtailed down the road in the opposite direction of Will. The acrid smell of burning rubber surrounded her.

Coughing and eyes watering, she sat up and waved away the suffocating cloud of dust.

Will stopped the patrol car next to her and jumped out. "What happened?"

"A truck came out of nowhere. Go after him." Annie pointed in the direction the truck went.

"You're my priority. You're bleeding. Are you okay?"

"Not sure." She held her palms up. Blood seeped from her dirty, torn skin. "I guess the chrome piece of evidence is messed up."

"We'll worry about that later. Let's get you cleaned up. There's a first aid kit in the patrol car."

He escorted her to the car and helped her sit down. Her knees stung. She ran her scraped hand across her dirt-encrusted skirt.

"Looks like your knees and right hand took the brunt of the fall." He gently cleaned the dirt from her legs and hands and swabbed the abrasions with alcohol. "Sting?"

"Yes." She winced and fanned her knees.

"This ointment will be more soothing." He handed her a tube. His kindness touched her heart.

She applied the salve to the sore spots and handed it back. "Thank you."

Will replaced the supplies in the kit and snapped the lid closed. "Can you tell me what happened, exactly?"

She did not miss the fact he'd made certain she was okay before he dealt with business. Closing her eyes, Annie pulled up the image of the truck bearing down on her. "It felt like the truck just dropped out of the sky with the engine roaring. Judging from the angle he came at me, he must have come from that side road." She pointed to the right. "Then he gunned it."

"Is it possible he entered the highway and saw you at the last minute, maybe blinded by sun glare, then swerved to miss you?"

"I ... I don't know. It happened so fast. If he barely missed running over me by accident, why didn't he stop?"

Will retrieved the metal trim piece. Part of it had been flattened. "Do you think it was the same truck that forced you off the road?"

She grimaced. "You're going to get tired of hearing this. I don't know."

She fought against her ineptitude. She couldn't think of one thing she could say for sure about the incident other than she had been shocked and scared witless. She'd always seen herself as competent in the face of sudden disaster and believed she'd make an exceptionally observant witness. Those thoughts did not allow for internal hysteria.

"Annie, level with me. Is there a reason someone is trying to harm you?"

She shook her head, but uncertainty made the bottom drop from her stomach.

On the way back to the sheriff's office, Will scrutinized the side roads ahead and in the rearview mirror, looking for the phantom truck. Annie had shaken her head and raised her bandaged right hand as if to say she had no idea why she might be someone's target. He'd been in law enforcement nine years. His job was to protect her, but something about her sent troubling vibes he could not pinpoint.

She was scuffed up, troubled, and ... cute. He wasn't supposed to feel that way about a complainant. She pushed golden brown hair away from her face only to have a strand giving off a sweet lavender scent fall forward.

"Thank you for taking time for me."

"No problem."

"Those words are nice to hear, but I always wonder about the truth behind them."

He glanced at her.

She swept her bandaged hand across her skinned knees in Vanna White game show hostess fashion like she'd given him plenty of reasons to view her as problematic.

"I'm just glad I was there to help you ... truly." The edges of her upturned mouth gave his heart a bump.

As they reached Sugarville, Annie stirred at the sight of a hot pink sign advertising the Sweet County fair. "The Confection Fair is this weekend. You should come."

"Thanks for the invite, but I don't know if I'll still be here."

"In case you are, I'm helping set up two of the booths. Sweet Nothin's Hair and Wear is offering free combs good for a ten percent discount, and my boss at the café will have free fudge samples."

Amazing. The girl had two attempts on her life and still has the presence of mind to promote the county fair. "I'll keep those offers in mind." Will reached the sheriff's office, pulling past Annie's car. "Why did you park on the side of the road?"

"I didn't want to block parking with the tree sticking out from under my car."

"Thoughtful."

He parked, and Annie reached for the door handle.

"Wait, I'll help you out."

"Thank you, but I can still function."

She was out of the door before he made it around the car. Did she take his offer as a sign that he saw her as weak? To the contrary, she struck him as someone who would rather run a marathon with a thorn in her foot than to slow down and remove it. "I left my jacket inside," she said.

He grabbed his investigations case off the back seat. "I'll gather evidence from your car while you get your jacket."

Will took photos of the damage to the Fiesta, gathered paint scrapings in a small bottle and attached an identification label. He caught a whiff of gasoline when he freed the trapped tree and tossed it next to bushes in the parking lot.

"Winnie said you have some calls to return," Annie said, coming back outside.

"No word from Sheriff Goutter?"

"I guess not."

Will glanced at his watch and scowled. Goutter had been gone over four hours.

"Thanks for getting the tree out of my bumper." A smile skated across her face. She opened her car door and tossed the jacket on the front seat.

"There's still debris under your car."

"No worries. You got the tree out. I'll deal with the other stuff later." She slid into the front seat. "Do you smell gas?"

Will walked to the driver's side. The gas smell was strong. "Hold up." He stooped to get a closer look. Clumps of dried grass and tree refuse below the gas tank were soaked in gasoline. Her car had a gas leak.

In his peripheral vision, he saw a passing truck's metal bumper struck the pothole. Sparks shot out. The gas leak ignited, and the line of fire headed straight for Annie's car.

"Out of the car!" Will yanked her off the seat and with a powerful shove sent her stumbling into the bushes. Snatching her jacket off the seat, he threw it down and stomped out the flame. The fibers of the jacket sizzled and shriveled. Smoke billowed up making his nose and eyes water.

He wiped at his face with his forearm and turned to Annie. "Are you okay?"

"I ... think ..."Annie raised to her knees, pushing the hair out of her eyes.

Winnie poked her head out of the office door. "Did I see smoke out here? What in the world happened?"

"We almost had early July 4th fireworks." Will helped Annie stand to her feet.

"With my car." Annie batted at the dirt stuck to her clothing with her bandaged hands.

"The gas tank must have been damaged when you were run off the road. You left a trail of gasoline." Will blew out a heavy sigh. "Sorry about your jacket, but it turned out to be a lifesaver."

Annie picked pine needles from her hair. "I can replace the jacket a lot easier than the car."

The bandages Will had applied earlier were now blood soaked and dirty. "Winnie, can you help Annie clean up?"

"That's okay. I have to go to work."

"Why not call work and say you can't come in?" Winnie said.

"I already took off this morning. I can't let Candy down. And my car—"

Will held up a hand. "Don't worry. Wash up, and I'll take you to work. Winnie, do you know a good auto repairman who can fix Annie's gas tank?"

"Call Gus Braxton. He's in the phone book. Come inside, honey. I keep Band-Aids in my purse for these unexpected occasions." Winnie guided Annie up the steps, then turned to speak over her shoulder. "Phone messages for you are on the desk, and I just heard a fax coming in."

As the two disappeared inside, Will's mind filled with questions. Were the incidents involving Annie deliberate, accidental, or a combination? Annie was certain she was run off the road on purpose, she narrowly missed being run over, and now her car had a gasoline leak. But topping his list of questions—where was Sheriff Goutter?

Will dusted his dirty hands against his slacks and went inside to deal with the phone messages. There had been an inquiry about gun-carrying laws. A report of a barking dog that Winnie referred to the police department. His eyes settled on a call to return from Craig Dillavey at the governor's office. He placed the call.

"Craig Dillavey," a man's voice answered.

"Will Brice in Sweet County. I had a note to call you?"

"Yes. The governor asked I call and inform you that you've been appointed acting sheriff."

There were voices in the background and faint laughter. Just the kind of stunt the state agents he'd been working with would cook up during their downtime. "Enough with the jokes. Tell the guys they have crime to fight."

"What's that? Sorry for the noise, but I'm at a reception with the governor."

"I said, I'm not falling for your joke."

"This is no joke. Ray Goutter is in the hospital with acute appendicitis. Before he went into surgery, he resigned and said you were more than able to run things. I sent you a fax."

"Hold on." Will pulled the latest fax from the tray. The message read:

Will Brice, you are hereby appointed Sheriff of Sweet County, Florida. This communication is to serve as your official authority to perform the duties of sheriff until a special election is held according to the election statutes of the county. Claude Renfroe, Jr, Governor.

Will's jaw muscle twitched, and his limbs went numb.

Winnie emerged from the restroom, Annie at her side with fresh bandages. He pinched his lips together and turned the paper around for them to see. His vision of working alongside seasoned officers vanished with the words on the paper.

He continued the conversation on the phone. "I have your fax, but I respectfully suggest you appoint someone who lives around here. At least this county was part of Goutter's jurisdiction. I'm an outsider, a sure recipe for failure."

"The only way you'll fail is if you turn down the job. Frankly, the governor wants an outsider rather than entrusting the position to someone from Sweet County. Governor Renfroe will meet with you at eleven o'clock Monday morning."

Stunned, Will hung up.

"Are you our new sheriff?" Winnie asked.

"I'm afraid so."

CHAPTER 4

Annie clipped breakfast orders from customers seated at the tables on the pulley rope, sending them to Candy in the kitchen. She tightened the sash on the pink ruffled *Candy's Café* bib-apron that had come loose. The aroma of freshly brewed coffee and sizzling bacon, normally yummy to her senses, gnawed at her stomach.

Yesterday's crazy events tumbled in her head, including the unhappy expression on Will's face when he received the appointment as sheriff. But today's irritation came from the insurance adjuster.

Annie refilled the coffee mugs of her counter customers—Jessie Simpson and Lessie Putman, twin sister operators of Sweet Nothin's Hair and Wear, and Bob Kittrell, owner of Bob's Barber Shop. They were regulars who ate breakfast at Candy's before opening their businesses.

"The whole system of car insurance stinks."

"Why does insurance stink?" Lessie asked.

"Some maniac ran me off the road, and the adjuster estimates fifteen hundred dollars in damages. I have a fifteen-hundred-dollar deductible." She flipped her palms up in frustration, exposing her bandaged hands. "Which means I foot the entire bill. Through no fault of my own, I have a banged up car that almost exploded because of a hole in the gas tank. My rates could even go up. It's not fair."

Jessie stirred sugar into her coffee, the spoon clinking against the sides of the cup. "I heard you were forced off the road and later almost run over. But what's this about an explosion?"

"You ladies at Sweet Nothin's are slippin'," Bob said. "A spark caught the gas leak on fire, and the new sheriff stomped it out."

"With my new suit jacket."

"Bring me your skirt." Lessie instructed, "I'll match the fabric and sew another jacket for you."

Candy rang the bell, announcing an order was ready for pick-up, and Annie took the breakfast plates to Juanita Freund and Sara Jane Gilley at the window table.

"Is the gas leak on your car fixed?" Sara Jane peppered her eggs. "With gas prices like they are, I'd hate to lose a drop."

"Yes, ma'am. Will had it fixed and my car delivered to the parsonage." Annie deposited extra napkins on their table and returned to the counter.

"Will." Bob wiggled his brows. "You're on a first name basis?"

Annie narrowed her eyes. "You'd be using his first name, too, if he'd kept your car from exploding. Now I'm out fifteen hundred dollars, and a demonic guy is on the loose."

Bob motioned for Jessie to pass the blueberry jam. "Don't you hate it when you believe something but can't prove it?"

"Yeah, like I know Bob puts color on his hair, but I can't prove it." Jessie winked and pushed the jar of jam in his direction.

"Don't be startin' false rumors." Bob spooned jam on his toast. "Annie, some things grow out of proportion in your mind when you dwell on them."

"You think I'm imagining being run off the road? I am not mistaken." Annie resupplied the sugar packet container with a vengeance.

"Bob. Leave her alone," Lessie said. "She saw what she saw."

"I will if I get a refill." Bob held up his coffee cup.

Annie grabbed the coffeepot, gave Bob a refill, and put a clamp on her uncharitable attitude. She could stand to learn from Lessie about smoothing troubling issues. Still, the heat of unfairness had her riled.

Chief Woodham entered the rear café door from Pie Street and bellowed, "We have another new sheriff, Daly's replacement quit already."

Candy emerged from the warm kitchen, pushing the fringe of bangs off her forehead with the back of her hand.

"Chief, we know that already."

"But did you know he's twenty-nine?" The chief slid onto a free stool at the counter. "Fix me a coffee to go, Candy. I can't stay."

"Bless Bess," Juanita said. "Twenty-nine. Isn't that too young for such a big job?"

Sara Jane flicked at a speck of lint on her sleeve. "Young or old, I'd say it's about time somebody cleaned house."

Farm equipment businessman Al Redfern came in the front door and sat at the counter. Paramedics Michael and Drew arrived after him and sat at a table while the café banter continued.

"Turn over a few logs in Sweet County and you might expose all kinds of critters." Juanita sniffed her hawkish nose.

"I don't know," Candy said. "Sometimes when you stir things up, it only makes things worse."

"What makes things worse?" Mr. Redfern asked.

"We're talking about the governor firing our sheriff. I'm not sure I like the idea of some out-of-town appointee taking over," Candy said.

"Sheriff Daly may have allowed some things to go on that he shouldn't have," Bob added, "but he knew everybody."

"Yup. I've never seen anyone remember names like he could. See y'all later." Chief Woodham waved as he exited with his coffee.

Annie took water and menus to the paramedics and returned to the counter.

"I understand we have a young appointee now," Mr. Redfern said.

"Young but competent," Annie said. She filled a coffee mug and slid it in front of Mr. Redfern.

"You know this? How?"

Annie detailed yesterday's hair raising events.

"You must have been frightened."

"Very."

Mr. Redfern was the first person to show any real sympathy.

"Did you get the tag number on that truck?"

"No. All I know is the truck is white and had a red bumper sticker on the back, at least part of one. I intend to find the guy and make him pay my repair bill."

"I know a guy who does auto body work at his house and is reasonable. I'll give you his name and number." Mr. Redfern wrote on the back of a business card and handed it to her.

"Thanks." Annie pocketed the card in her apron and watched Mr. Redfern stack three sugar packets together, rip off the tops, and pour the sweetener into his coffee. "You put the sweet in Sweet County in more ways than one."

Michael held up his menu. "We'll come back for lunch. Just bring us coffee for now."

Annie took cups and the coffeepot to their table.

"How did it go at the governor's office yesterday?" Michael asked.

"You heard about my interview?" Annie asked, filling their mugs.

"Word travels fast in this town," Candy said with a hint of pride. "My café relays news way quicker than the *Sugarville Weekly Journal*."

"You've got stiff competition from Bob's Barber Shop." Mr. Redfern said and sipped his coffee.

"Don't forget Sweet Nothin's Hair and Wear." Juanita raised her chin to add to the friendly rivalry.

"Stiff competition. Y'all have me there," Candy conceded.

"To answer your question," Annie said to Michael, "the interview went well, but they might fill the job internally. You two staying busy?"

"Dealing with high schoolers and their poor decisions," Michael said.

"Except we normally deal with them on Friday nights," Drew said.

"Are you talking about the Thornton accident on Old Water Tower Road yesterday?"

Drew nodded. "Being employed here has you on top of the latest."

Annie didn't explain she'd first heard of the accident at the sheriff's office because he was right. Bob Kittrell opened the morning's counter discussion with the Thornton mishap. "You say Friday nights are your busiest?"

"Fridays are generally known as unhinged."

"Why unhinged?"

Drew waved his hand back and forth like a fish tail. "Illegal drug and alcohol sales get so busy; the suppliers' doors nearly swing off the hinges."

"Wouldn't it be easier to be a wet county?"

"Not for teens or suppliers. Teens can access booze, and suppliers have no costly license to lose."

"Do you think the Thornton accident involved teen drinking?"

Michael stirred creamer into his coffee and turned down the volume of his voice. "Mrs. Thornton told the highway patrolman at the hospital the driver was young, had a flushed face, and looked dazed. Sounds like drinking or drugs."

"Or both," Drew added.

Annie set the coffeepot and herself down at their table. "I was the victim of a hit-and-run yesterday too. Fifteen-hundred-dollars worth of damage. Can you tell me more about these places with swinging doors? If the culprit frequents these places, maybe I can find him."

"Hey, Annie," Candy called to her. "I need you to put on another pot of coffee."

"Oops." Annie stood, grasped the near empty pot and hurried back behind the counter.

Candy's wrinkled forehead and hoarse whisper revealed her displeasure. "A word to the wise. It's better to keep your ears open and limit what comes from your mouth. Sugarville is a pretty sweet place to live if you don't ask too many questions."

Annie opened her mouth, then closed it.

With the breakfast shift ended and the town's news thoroughly chewed and stirred, Annie headed to her car. She rolled her shoulders, relieving the tension. Waitressing called for not only physical stamina but mental smarts to get orders out quickly and as requested.

She'd annoyed her employer and would have to be more careful. Reaching her car, she found an envelope stuck in the window on the driver's door. Cautiously, she opened the envelope and pulled out the contents—fifteen one-hundred-dollar bills with a handwritten note attached.

Here's the money to fix your car. For your own good, don't pursue the matter further.

Sitting at the worn desk inside the small office with "Sheriff" printed on the door, Will hung up the phone and kneaded tense muscles in his neck. He'd been on the phone all morning, peddling sworn officer jobs loaded with questionable benefits. Come work questionable hours, for questionable pay, for a questionable period in Sweet County—a unique, bundled employment package. And the offer comes from a temporary sheriff who does not want the position.

Winnie, who was covering the front desk, announced on the intercom. "Call from Buzz Sinclair on line one."

Will picked up.

"Have you got things running smoothly in Sweet County yet?" Buzz asked. "I don't like being the only greenhorn for the seasoned guys to pick on down here."

"Trust me. I'd rather have state guys hazing me than stepping in as Sheriff of Sweet County. The former sheriff left

41

nothing, and I mean nothing, of value to work with here." Will scanned the gray walls with light-gray, rectangular shapes where pictures had been removed and the line of inaccessible gray metal file cabinets. "I have no keys, supplies, deputies, or dispatchers. The police department is loaning me a clerk. I've been on the phone all morning trying to recruit help."

"No kidding? My friend, I hate to say it, but I'm glad you were picked and not me. I called to make sure you knew the latest. It's rumored FDLE is going to only accept agents with degrees from certified programs. The on-line course we took was rigorous but hasn't been approved for accreditation."

Will's chest tightened. He swiveled his chair around, giving him a view of the rear gravel lot and the 1960s-era Sweet Dreams Motel on the adjacent street. "What if we're currently with the agency?"

"Our first year is probationary. I hope we'll be grandfathered in. But with your appointment as sheriff and interruption of service, who knows? My advice—wrap things up as soon as you can and rejoin me. I need the relief."

Relief is what Will needed. Hopefully, the county supervisor of elections would schedule a special election for sheriff soon.

Winnie stepped into his office, brandishing her phone message book. "Want some good news?"

"I'm ready."

"PeeWee and Cheryl Norton will be here around noon tomorrow."

"That is good news."

"And Pee Wee said to tell you Tommy-something is coming too. He hung up before I could ask him to repeat the last name."

Will felt a surge of heartburn. "Singletree, maybe?"

Winnie ripped the message from the pad and handed it to him. "Could be. I think it started with an S." The phone rang, taking her back to the reception desk.

Will fanned the note across his fingertips. Winnie's conversation with the current caller faded into the background. He should be thankful for an extra volunteer, but Tommy Singletree could be a handful. At this point, he had to welcome any lawman willing to work. As incentive, he'd promised the jail living quarters where he had slept last night to Pee Wee and his wife and needed to clear his things out.

"Winnie, I'll be in the back."

He walked down the hallway behind the reception area, past iron-barred jail cells, and entered the apartment across from the jail kitchen.

The living quarters consisted of an efficiency kitchen with a small living area, bedroom, and bath. The room still carried the strong formaldehyde odor of the new sheets he'd purchased at the dollar store. He should have purchased a pillow too. The lumpy jail feather pillow smelled musty, even with a new pillowcase. The dank odor took him back twenty years to Hill County and the nightmarish memory of crying muffled tears into his pillow the night his mother died.

He yanked the sheets from the bed, hating the smells and the recollection. He'd vowed to never return to Hill County, and Sweet County was too close for comfort.

He rolled the sheets in a wad and started back down the hallway. Next problem—where was he going to stay? The Sweet Dreams Motel had a vacancy sign. He'd try it and hope the place delivered on its name.

Returning to the front office, Winnie pressed the hold button and held up the phone. "Better take this call, it's about the Confection Fair."

Will nodded. "Transfer the call to my office." He tossed the bundled sheets into the corner and picked up. "Will Brice. Can I help you?"

"This is John Stenneson, the manager of the fairgrounds. Is this the new sheriff?"

"Yes, sir."

"The Sweet County Confections Fair opens at four o'clock tomorrow and will run Friday and Saturday evenings. The sheriff's office has always been in charge of security. Can I count on you?"

Will looked at the lone photo left hanging on the sheriff's wall, depicting an aerial view of the Sweet County fairgrounds. Will had worked fairs in Duval County and was familiar with the needs. "I am short on staff, but help is to arrive tomorrow. I'll come by early afternoon."

"Great. I'll look for you then."

Will jotted down a meeting reminder and made a mental note to check the location of the fairgrounds.

Winnie used the intercom to tell him line two was holding for him. He punched the button. "Sheriff Brice."

"Sheriff? That has a nice ring to it. This is Tommy. Tommy Singletree. Did you hear I'm coming to help you?"

Tommy was a big burly deputy. He had a soft heart but didn't know his own strength. He'd fight at the drop of a hat and sometimes dropped the hat. But the 'beggars can't be choosers' saying fit this occasion.

"Yes, Tommy, I did. But understand, I can't guarantee how long you'll have the job."

"Sure. I understand. However long you need me. Rest easy 'cause I've got your back."

With that assurance, Will was in for another restless night. He penned another note to call insurance about personal bonds for his officers.

"Knock, knock."

He looked up. Annie. The flutter in his stomach at seeing her bright smile and hearing the sound of her voice surprised him.

"Winnie said you just got off the phone. Okay to come in?"

"Certainly. How are your wounds today?"

She held up her bandaged hands, a paper sack grasped in one. "Sore but okay. I hear from Winnie you have help coming."

"I do. A retired police officer and his wife agreed to come and stay at the jail, and another man who serves in the Duval County auxiliary is coming." He pointed to the sack in her hand. "Did you pack a lunch?"

"No. It's related to my case, and I thought I should show it to you. I got a bag and borrowed tongs from the café to keep from handling it too much in case you can get fingerprints."

She had his attention.

Setting the bag on his desk and using the tongs, she pulled out an envelope with cash and a handwritten note. He read the note, then asked, "How much cash is in there?"

"Fifteen hundred."

"How would anyone know the amount you needed to fix your car?"

"After the insurance adjuster gave me an estimate," she wrinkled her nose, "I kind of complained at the café about what it was costing and said I wanted to find the guy. It is only fair he pays to fix my car."

"Kind of complained? Who was there?"

Annie tapped her finger against her lips. "Let me see. There was Candy, of course. At the counter was Jessie and Lessie from Sweet Nothin's, Bob Kittrell, the barber, Juanita and Sara Jane, they're regulars."

Will closed his eyes and started shaking his head, but looked back up when she kept going.

"Then Chief Woodham, Al Redfern, a couple of paramedics. A few others came in, but once the tables were full, there was little time for talking. Those are the main ones who heard me complain."

"And of course, any of those people could have shared the information outside the café."

"At first, I thought it might be someone trying to help me out."

"But whoever it was included a threat."

"Unfortunately, the threat negates the good deed."

"I'm impressed with your precautions."

She folded her arms across her chest and sighed, "Thanks."

Bringing him the cash and note was commendable. "What made you consider fingerprint preservation?"

She tugged a tendril of hair. "I watch a lot of *Law and Order*."

She drifted from confident to a bit uptight.

"I'll keep this as evidence along with the trim we recovered and take your fingerprints for elimination prints."

"That won't be necessary. My prints are on file with the state."

"Why?"

The hesitation to respond was slight, but she did hesitate.

"To apply for the PR job at the governor's office, fingerprints were required."

Her explanation made sense, but not the feeling he picked up on when she paused.

"Fine. The forensic lab will have access. In the meantime, do something for me."

"If I can."

"Don't broadcast you are after this guy to make him pay. Someone doesn't want the driver of that truck known, and I want to find out why."

CHAPTER 5

The Sweet County Confections Fair bustled with the chatter of locals preparing booths and the clanging and pounding noises of carnival workers assembling the amusements.

Annie whacked the stapler against the wooden table edge while Lessie held the pleated pink fabric in place. "Ouch." Annie turned her hands palms up and blew on the abrasions. "I don't recommend using hands for brakes."

"Let's trade jobs." Lessie took the stapler, and Annie held the fabric in place.

"Annie, I hate you are having such a rough start in Sweet County," Jessie said as she set up folding chairs. "Sugarville is supposed to leave a sweet taste, pun intended."

"No worries. I have been sniffing fudge Candy is making for the fair for the last two days, and now I'm breathing in the tasty aroma coming from the cooking contestants. If the sweet smells deliver on taste, all is well." Annie nodded in the direction of the pie baking contest, then stopped to stare at a girl escorting a chubby pink pig. His snout tilted upward. "Looks like I'm not the only one sniffing. Is there a pig contest?"

Jessie chuckled. "If there is, Jelly Bean will be a spectator, not a contestant."

"He's the Forehand's pet pig," Lessie said, and waved the girl over. "Nettie Sue, I see Jelly Bean has a new outfit."

The pig, whose ears stood out like flags caught in the wind, wore a blue plaid collar with a "Sweet as Pie" button attached.

"Yessum. I made the collar from a child's discarded rain boots."

"Annie, meet Nettie Sue Forehand. She is Sugarville's master of making treasures out of trash. Annie is the daughter of the new preacher at Community Church."

"Pleased to meet you," Annie said. "Your pig is adorable."

"Thanks." Nettie Sue was polite but smileless. "I come to set up my crafts." She pointed to an exhibit space a few tables down. "I'll be giving away the Sweet as Pie buttons. Could Jelly Bean sit with you? I'll be coming and going, and he hates to be left alone."

Jelly Bean sniffed Annie's shoes, plunked down beside her, and rested his flat snout on her foot.

Nettie Sue's forehead wrinkled, and she scratched her head. "Ain't that somethin'. He usually has to warm up to a stranger."

"We'll watch him for you," Jessie said.

Nettie kept eyeing her pig. "Ain't never seen it—him takin' to somebody so quick." She left, shaking her head.

Annie watched Nettie Sue's departure, afraid to move her foot.

"Since Nettie's mother passed away, Jelly Bean can't stand to be by himself," Jessie explained. "She had her bangs trimmed at the shop last week and brought Jelly Bean with her. Jelly Bean laid right beside the barber chair the whole time. He is a well-behaved pig."

"Jessie, take over holding the fabric so we don't disturb Jelly Bean all comfy on Annie's foot," Lessie directed.

The two continued working on the table edging. The pig made a soft grunt that came out like a sigh and twitched his ears.

"Nettie's had little formal education but creates wonderful items from things people throw away," Jessie said. "She makes daily trips to the county dump, and Jelly Bean helps her root out trash for her treasures. The girl is talented. Even fashions the custom pin-back buttons like the one Jelly Bean's wearing."

"She never finished school?"

"An old farming tradition—if parents needed their kids' help on the farm, the school didn't interfere."

"But this is the twenty-first century, and she looks to be twenty something. Don't you have truancy officers?"

"Maybe, but this is Sweet County. Things are dealt with differently here."

Someone called Annie's name. She turned to see Will walking over, and her pulse rate kicked up a notch. After introducing Jessie and Lessie, Jelly Bean grunted and rolled over on his side, freeing Annie's foot.

"Is he your pig?" Will asked Annie.

"No, sir." Lessie interceded. "Jelly Bean is an icon around town, and he took a shine to Annie." Lessie made the proclamation as if Annie had been bestowed a great honor.

Heat flushed Annie's face.

Will's expression lit up. "I congratulate you on receiving the admiration of a town celebrity."

"Thank you, I think. He probably relates to me since I've spent time on all fours of late and he can whiff good food smells on my shoes from Candy's café."

"I just set up security for this evening with the fair manager and thought I'd tour the grounds."

"As sheriff, you need to be familiar with the fair and the town," Lessie said. "Art Redfern is setting up his carriage ride by the back parking lot. Annie, we have things under control here. Tell Art the other set of twins said to give you the Sugarville grand tour."

"Other set of twins?"

"Art's twin is Al, you met at the café. Jess and I were in the same grade in school."

"But what about Jelly Bean?"

Jelly Bean sat up and blinked his black eyes lined with light pink lashes at her.

"We'll take care of him and let Nettie Sue know you were concerned." Lessie shooed them away.

"Sorry for the obvious manipulation." Annie glanced back over her shoulder. "I've never had an animal attach to me like he did. Silly ... but it feels nice."

"Not silly, acceptance is a human need. I suppose it extends to pigs. If you'd rather not go, I'll do my best to understand you chose Jelly Bean's company over mine."

"Oh ... it's not that I don't want to—"

His serious tone melded into a friendly smile.

A pleasant feeling spread over her. "You are messing with me."

They stepped from the exhibit hall to where the big open field had transformed into a carnival midway, complete with calliope music and the scent of salted popcorn.

"Yup. Messing with you, just like these smells, sights, and sounds mess with fairgoers, enticing them to participate."

A uniformed deputy waved and approached. Will introduced her to Tommy Singletree. The man looked at least six-and-a-half-feet tall and could go shoulder to shoulder with any pro football lineman.

"Boss, since we're short on equipment, the fair manager is charging walkie talkies for us to use on the fairgrounds."

"Good. I'm going on a town tour and will pick one up when I return. In the meantime, I have my cell phone if you need me. I won't be long."

"Yes, sir. I'll handle things here till you get back."

Annie led the way to the carriage stand near the rear parking lot. Easy to spot, Art Redfern wore traditional carriage driver clothing, including a dark gray sport coat and slacks topped with a bowler-style hat.

After introductions, Annie explained, "Since we're new to town, the other twins said to tell you to give us the Sugarville grand tour before the fair gets underway."

Art chuckled. "Jess and Less know I'll take care of you." He led them to a black leather carriage with glossy lacquered wheels attached to a dapple-gray horse decorated with pink tasseled fringe.

A young man with blonde curly hair anchored by a cap pulled low on his brow spoke with concern. "Cupcake is acting mighty funny. When I hold up a carrot, she always takes it but not now. She must be sick."

Art answered in an edgy tone. "She's got on blinders. It limits her view."

"Oh ... yeah." He patted the horse's back. "I guess so."

Art slipped from cordial to annoyed and back again. "Folks settle in." He held out his hand and helped Annie in the carriage. Will climbed in behind her. Once settled in the carriage, Art clicked his tongue, and they were rolling.

Leaving the busyness of the fairgrounds, Art said, "We'll be taking the less traveled Old Confection Street into town. Cupcake knows this road by heart."

The horse plodded along, keeping a slow, regular, clippity-clop cadence. Annie prayed the slowed pace would help put Will at ease since the governor had turned his life upside down by appointing him sheriff.

"Sweet County derives its name from the sweet corn and sugarcane grown in the area. You will notice all the streets of Sugarville bear names of something sweet."

Their tour took them by the country club and golf course, where President Hoover had played a round of golf in 1932. The stately 1917 courthouse with a silver dome and clock sat in the middle of town. Quaint shops and eateries with matching awnings of pink and burgundy surrounded the square.

"The gazebo on the courthouse lawn is referred to as nuptial corner because of the large number of soldiers who tied the knot there before shipping off during World War II. Some folks wanted to tear down the courthouse and build a new one, but we stopped that foolishness."

"It's nice that the citizens care enough to preserve the history," Annie said.

"You'll find that merchants in Sugarville band together on lots of things. We're one of the few dry counties left. No service or sales of alcohol in any establishments in the county," Art said with some pride.

"Dry counties don't eliminate drinking problems," Will said.

Art cleared his throat. "Kids will be kids. At least it's not out in the open."

"You have a point," Will said. "Bars and honky-tonks produce frequent calls to law enforcement for fighting and other disturbances."

"My argument exactly. Being dry makes Sugarville and the county visibly inviting. You'll see once you become a part of our little community."

Moving along Molasses Street, Cupcake automatically veered back onto Sugar Avenue.

"Told you. Cupcake knows this route. We've come full circle."

The ride had been informative and pleasurable. With Will at her side and the hypnotic clip clop of the horse's hooves on the pavement, Annie hated for the tour to end. But Cupcake dutifully turned back onto the fairgrounds where a long line awaited admission.

After thanking Art for the tour, Will and Annie went in opposite directions.

"Annie. Thank goodness you're back. It's so hot out here, I had to pack the pans of fudge in ice." Candy hauled in a breath, perspiration beaded her forehead. "Go to my car and get the coupons on the front seat and finish helping me set up the table before the gates open."

Candy steered Annie toward the parking lot and dropped car keys in her hand. "Hurry, please."

Annie spotted Candy's maroon Jeep Cherokee parked midway in the lot, but a white truck matching the description of the one that rammed into her caught her attention.

She circled the truck, which had more than a few dents and scratches. There was no bumper sticker on the back fender, but one could have been removed. She took out her phone and snapped a shot of the tag, which had a glob of dried mud concealing the last number. She knelt to rub the dirt away.

"What are doing?"

The gruff voice startled her. Losing her balance, Annie sat down hard on the ground and looked up into the face of a man she had served at the café. "Mr. Beck, hello. I was just—"

"Getting my tag number? What for?" He bent over, leaning in close enough for her to catch a hint of alcohol mixed with the aroma of his sweat-stained shirt. "Am I parked wrong?"

Annie maneuvered to her knees.

"No, I—"

"If I did, what concern is it of yours? I don't appreciate you snooping around my truck."

"No, sir."

"Annie, what's taking so long?" Candy barked her irritation. "Why are you on the ground?" She looked from Annie to Mr. Beck. "Hi, Vernon. A problem here?"

"Ask her. She's taking down my tag number."

"I ... this truck looks like the one that ran me off the road."

"What?" The word shot out of Mr. Beck's mouth like a rock from a slingshot. Color crept up his neck and spread to his ears. "I came straight from the field, hauling my watermelons. Never come close to a soul."

"It didn't happen today." Annie stood dusting dirt from her rear end. "But obviously it wasn't you ... sorry."

He harrumphed. "I've never been accused of such."

"Of course not," Candy said and patted him on the shoulder. "We look forward to your watermelons every year. I plan to feature them on the menu in June."

"Good." He nodded to Candy, then swept his irritated gaze over Annie. He climbed into his truck, fired up the engine and backed out, chugging from the lot in a puff of oily smelling smoke.

"Annie," her name came out of Candy's mouth with as much derision as she'd received from Mr. Beck. "I can't have you upsetting my customers."

"But I didn't—"

"—think. You didn't think. I cannot be any clearer. If you want to stay on Sugarville's sweet side, let law enforcement handle your investigation."

Two hours after the gates opened, the call from Stenneson came over the walkie talkie. "Sheriff, we've got a problem at the shooting gallery."

Will keyed the handheld radio. "Where's my deputy?"

"He's in the middle of the melee."

On the breath of an urgent prayer to please have no one get hurt, Will weaved through the crowd of fairgoers enjoying grilled hot dogs and cotton candy. Spotting a group of curious onlookers, they stepped back when Will arrived, letting him through.

"I've never seen anything to match it," a heavy-set man in overalls said. "He just picked up them boys, one in each hand, knocked their heads together and tossed 'em to the ground like they were sacks of potatoes."

"Redferns and Becks at it again," came another comment.

In the clearing, Will saw Tommy hoist one limp body over his shoulder. Visions of lawsuits danced in his head.

"Sheriff, I tried. I tried real hard to talk to them."

"Okay, folks, break it up. Show's over. Enjoy the rest of the fair," Will said. The spectators gradually dispersed.

Tommy shook his head and adjusted the weight of the man on his shoulder. "I'm taking him to the patrol car, and I'll be right back for the other one. They wouldn't listen."

The carny at the shooting booth agreed. "That boy there," he pointed to the one still on the ground, "he accused the other one of cheating him out of his teddy bear. But the other fella won the bear fair and square. I think stimulants interfered, if you know what I mean."

The man on the ground had disheveled blond hair and a familiar face. It was the young man who was concerned about the horse not eating. The remains of a teddy bear lay on the ground with its head ripped off and stuffing scattered. "Looks like neither one will take the bear home," Will said.

Tommy returned. He hoisted the limp man to his shoulder and carted him to the patrol car. Will picked up teddy bear remains and spoke to the concession operator. "We'll provide a place for them to sleep it off at the county jail."

"Appreciate it. That big deputy of yours doesn't play around."

"No, he doesn't." Tommy was good at crowd control, but he could deliver a strong wallop and had to be cautioned and reminded of the damage he could inflict.

When Will reached the patrol car, Tommy was closing the door to the cage area. "I think one of 'em is rousing."

"I don't belong in no cage," came a voice from the back seat.

Tommy rapped on the window. "You do now. Keep quiet. Boss, I know you said to be careful. I don't want to cause you any problems with the governor and all, but they kept scuffling. With the folks gathering around, I was afraid someone else might get hurt."

"It's okay, especially if you felt they were endangering others. Take them to the jail, and let Pee Wee book them."

New shouts rose in the crowd behind him. What now? He turned to see Lessie waving her arms to get his attention. "Come quick. Annie's in trouble."

"Snoopin' where you don't belong."

Will heard the man's voice clearly above the carnival noises and laughter from the people enjoying the fair. Partially visible between onlookers, he saw a man shove Annie.

Will pushed his way through the crowd. Annie was on the ground. He grabbed her attacker.

"Hey, I know what I saw. Just lettin' her know to lay off." The man flailed an arm haphazardly and breathed out a whiff of alcohol.

Will wrestled the man to the ground and handcuffed him. "And I'm just letting *you* know it's battery when you lay hands on someone."

Will used the portable radio to contact Tommy. "I've got one more for you to load when you return. Come to the food concessions beside the exhibit hall."

"Thank goodness you're here," Candy said. "Mr. Beck has it in his head Annie is trying to cause him trouble."

Will knelt beside Annie. "What trouble?"

Annie sat up. "I tried to apologize."

A bloody gash creased her arm. Will pulled out his handkerchief and wrapped it around the cut. "You have got to be the unluckiest person I've ever met. Looks like you'll need stitches."

"There's a clinic nearby," Lessie said. "I'll take her."

After they left, Candy filled him in on the incident.

"Vernon Beck is a good man, a hard worker, but alcohol changes his personality a might. When he saw Annie, he became agitated, called her a crazy woman, and said his proof was her moving into the Fleming house."

"Why does that make her crazy?"

"You're new here, but the house is said to be haunted. He's not the only one to think a person would be crazy to live there. Anyhow, he was already upset with Annie for getting his license plate number earlier."

"Why did Annie want his tag number?"

"She said his truck looked like the one that ran her off the road. She tried to explain and apologize, but Vernon said she wasn't fooling him. He claimed she was trying to tie him to illegal operations. Annie told him he was wrong, which made him angrier."

"What illegal operations?"

"Who knows?"

Candy's inflection bordered shrill. Will tabled that line of questioning. "Is that when he pushed her?"

"Yeah. It's like she poked a hornet's nest. Vernon said, 'Don't tell me I'm wrong,' and shouted other stuff, then pushed her. Annie grabbed for the table. The sharp end of the wire used to attach the fudge sign cut her arm when she fell." Candy pointed to the wire.

"Anything else you can tell me about the incident?"

Candy looked around and lowered her voice. "Just this. I told Annie after she took his tag number she needs to keep quiet and let you do the investigating."

CHAPTER 6

Monday. A new day. A new week. The fair was over, and Will longed for a new attitude.

After another restless night at the Sweet Dreams Motel, he sat at his desk, hands steepled beneath his chin, and assessed his situation. At eleven o'clock, he was to meet with the governor and be officially sworn in as sheriff of this strange county.

The fair had exposed a crusty layer of a Sweet County rivalry between the Becks and Redferns. Teddy bear brawler, J. W. Evans, woke up in jail Saturday morning, hungover, and received a chewing out from his uncle, Art Redfern.

The other teddy bear brawler, Hampton Beck, made the overnight jail stay a family event with his father, Vernon, who had assaulted Annie. One thing bound the adversaries together—inebriation.

Annie declined to file charges against Vernon, and Will had accepted her invitation to attend church on Sunday. His welcome at Community Church filled his weary, weighted soul, and he received a boost of grace to endure introductions and scrutiny after the service.

But now, looking out of his open office door, the effects of Sunday's message on resting in the security of the Lord in all circumstances diminished like the waning moon. Tommy, half sitting on the corner of Pee Wee's desk, munched from a box of Cracker Jack.

"Boss, tell this goon to get off my desk. He's chomping like a squirrel," Pee Wee complained.

Will shook his head and pushed out of his chair. What Tommy lacked in brilliance he made up for in brawn. And what Pee Wee lacked in height he made up for in spunk. These guys might be well-meaning, but he was in no mood to deal with silly squabbles.

While standing at the office door threshold, Will eyed the two.

Pee Wee straightened in his desk chair. Tommy slid his leg from the desk and stood.

"Lose the Cracker Jacks," Will said.

The box hit the metal trash can with a clang. "Sorry, boss."

"Tommy, I want you out driving the county. Be visible and ready if Pee Wee needs you to answer a call."

"Yes, sir." Tommy snapped his heels together, grabbed his Stetson, and headed for the door. "Be 10-8 in a jiffy."

Will sucked in air, resolute about his next steps. "Pee Wee, I'm going to get a haircut." He tapped the desk. "I'll walk. Call at the barber shop if you need anything."

Outside, the air was warm and humid. The shop with the spiraling barber pole sat a block away. Its burgundy and pink striped awning matched those of other downtown stores. Traffic was light, the town quiet. Climbing the slight incline, he felt a wave of responsibility. This was his county and his people to serve. But he hoped the time of service was short.

As he opened the barber shop door, a bell jingled. Inside smelled of fresh, lemony musk aftershave and clean smelling shampoo. A stocky man with thick, dark hair that would be the envy of a balding man was pulling on a white barber smock.

"Good morning. Are you Bob?"

"Guilty," he said, extending his hand. "Bob Kittrell. Are you the newly appointed sheriff?"

"Yes, sir. Will Brice, newly appointed and initiated by working the Sweet County Confection Fair."

A broad smile lifted round cheeks. "A big event in our community."

"Suppose I could get a haircut and shave? My official swearing in by the governor is later this morning, and I'd like to look presentable."

"You came to the right place." Bob patted the back of the barber chair.

Bob fastened a cape around his neck, splashed sweet smelling lotion in his hand and applied it to Will's face. "This will soften your beard for a clean shave while I work on your hair. So, you excited to be sheriff?"

"Stunned might be more descriptive. I was sent to assist the governor's appointee ... which turned out to be me."

"I can see where getting the appointment would be a shock—young as you are and all."

Though friendly on the surface, the age comment disclosed his cynicism. "Do you know where I can find Sheriff Daly? He's not listed in the phone book, and I have some questions concerning inventory. Hopefully, he'll talk to me."

"He's a personable guy. Experienced. You might as well know—a lot of people think he was wronged. He owns a place in town off Honey Dew Avenue. If he's not there, he could be at a friend's hunting cabin for some R & R." He nodded toward the front window. "Here's a man who might know."

The shop door opened and a big, broad-shouldered man with a cigar stub clenched in his teeth entered. "Howdy Bob. Dave ain't here yet?"

Bob combed and snipped Will's hair while he spoke. "Not yet. Meet our new sheriff, Will Brice."

"No kiddin'. I'm Hank Skinner." He stuck out his hand.

Will grasped his hand and received a tight squeeze.

"Our new sheriff wants to talk to Sheriff Daly. I heard he might have gone to one of those hunting cabins outside of town. You know where he might be?"

"Once, Sheriff Daly called me to bring the wrecker to a cabin he was stayin' in. That cabin's behind a locked gate, though, not a good place to go uninvited."

"Maybe I could leave a note on the gate for him to call me."

Hank took the unlit cigar stub from his mouth. "Maybe." The word came out short and clipped. "You go out the county road that runs by the old water tower to just before Goose Creek Hollow. Turn left. There are several unmarked roads with locked entries. The cabin where I pulled a vehicle out of the mud was at the end of the road. Ain't huntin' season, so he may or may not be there."

He shoved the cigar back in his mouth and sat in a chair beside a table with a checkerboard game box on top.

Had he touched a nerve with this man?

Bob turned the barber chair so Will faced the front window.

"Set up the checkerboard. Dave's here," Bob said.

The man who entered was thin, with pasty skin and droopy eyelids.

"Meet the new sheriff, Will Brice," Bob said. "Dave is a retired postal worker."

Dave offered a firm handshake. "Dave Barger. Sheriff, you're about to witness a dandy checkers match." The man took a seat opposite Hank and rubbed his hands together. "I'm feeling lucky today."

Hank shifted the cigar stub in his mouth. "The sheriff's got better things to do than hear your excuses when you lose to me today."

Bob worked at Will's sideburns. "Pay no attention to them. On Mondays, Sugarville likes to ease into the work week. Those retirees play checkers in the morning, but tradition is for downtown merchants to close up shop in the afternoon. Most head to the golf course."

Bob's razor buzzed along the nape of Will's neck.

"Having time off on Monday afternoons must make people look forward to the beginning of the week instead of dreading it."

"Sure does. I plan to go to the golf course this afternoon. Come out if you're back from the governor's office. It's a sure way to fit in."

"Fitting in is a good thing," Hank said. "You jump in and try to rock the boat, and ... well, you better fill him in on the history of sheriffs in this county."

Bob swished a brush in a shave cup and began smoothing cream on Will's face. "Over the years, we've had different sheriffs, but two in particular went to meddlin' into the town's customs."

"They found one in a secluded area, where he'd responded to a call." His razor slid skillfully over Will's cheek and jawline down to his neck. "The other had an unfortunate car accident crashing into the steep ravine coming into town off of the interstate. The governor had to appoint new sheriffs after those died," Hank said.

"You can pay your respects to your predecessors. They're pushing up daisies in the Sugarville Cemetery," Dave snickered.

"Who was it that said if you can't lick 'em, join 'em?" Hank hopped two spaces on the board. "Crown me ol' buddy. Still feelin' lucky?"

Discordant laughter swelled in the shop. Had he slipped into a macabre Floyd's Barber Shop from the old Andy Griffith TV show?

"Lay off you two." Bob unsnapped the cape around Will's neck and used a soft-bristled brush to dust off his collar.

Will slid out of the chair, pulled out his wallet, and paid Bob, leaving a decent tip. "Pleasure to meet everyone, but save your discourse on the fate of former sheriffs for the candidates who run for the office. In the meantime, I'd appreciate it if you would spread the word I'd like to speak to Sheriff Daly."

The jingling of the bell was the only sound coming from the shop when he walked out the door.

Still in her robe and slippers, Annie hummed the chorus of "God is my Strength," sung in yesterday's church service. She'd been hesitant to invite Will to church but pleased when he came.

The phone rang. Annie answered the wall-mounted kitchen phone with a tangled coil phone cord attached.

"Annie," her mother spoke loudly, as if the increased volume would help span the distance from Brazil to

Sugarville. "Your Dad's listening too. We had to arrange a ride into Macapà to call. We don't have phone service in the little village where we're working. Are you okay?"

Her father spoke. "Your message about the accident and damage to your car was relayed to us by our mission director."

A surge of nostalgia struck. She could picture them huddled together, sharing the phone. "Old news now."

She wouldn't mention being almost run over, or the near-car explosion, or the incident at the fair requiring stitches. "I'm fine. A crazy driver ran me off the road and dented the car, but it's drivable."

"Why would anyone force you off the road?" her mother asked.

"That's what I'd like to know," Annie tugged at the coil phone cord.

"Were you paying attention?" her dad asked.

"Maybe veered into their lane?" Her mother suggested.

Her dad came back with, "Did you report it?"

Annie closed her eyes. Some nostalgia was not so comforting. "I made a report at the sheriff's office and called the insurance adjuster. I'd like to find the guy who rammed me and make him pay for the damages." She'd not mention the cash offer accompanied by a cryptic note.

"Have it repaired and don't fret over who did it," her mother said.

"You were probably in his blind spot," came her dad's verdict.

Whenever a problem involved Annie, her parents always considered she might bear a measure of fault. In fairness, looking at both sides was the way her parents had handled their often-overzealous daughter's tendency to exaggerate and embellish. But she had learned to tone down her imagination over the years, and in this case, she saw what she saw. The man ran her off the road on purpose.

"I'm saving to meet the deductible, but enough about that. The guest preacher gave an excellent sermon, and the new sheriff came."

"What happened to the old sheriff?" her mother asked.

"The governor removed him from office. Something to do with allowing illegal activities to go on in the county."

"Don't you get involved," her dad said.

"What a thing to say." Her mother chided her dad. "I know you made the new sheriff feel welcome. You are fantastic at that."

"Yes, yes, you are." Her dad added, undoubtedly after being elbowed by her mother.

Annie's stitches stung. She'd try for a different subject. "Reverend Sewell preached a good sermon."

"Excellent. I hope you didn't sit in the front row. You tend to jiggle your leg." Her dad reverted to lecture mode. "You don't want to distract the guest preacher. It's tough enough preaching in a strange pulpit."

"Yes, Daddy. You trained me well. I took a seat a respectable few rows back. I plan to get the materials to tend to the rose garden today, and I set out rat traps in the basement. I keep hearing noises at night."

"We are so thankful you are there to watch after everything, dear."

Her father prayed before the call ended.

She swallowed against the knot in her throat and sniffed. Her mother and father were her fiercest critics but also her greatest cheerleaders.

The doorbell rang. Seven o'clock. Early for a visitor. Annie dabbed at her watery eyes, went to the door, and peeked out the security hole.

Nettie Sue Forehand?

Annie opened the door. Jelly Bean, sitting on his haunches with his front hooves positioned in perfect alignment, peered up at her. Beneath his pig nose, Annie could swear his mouth upturned in a smile.

Nettie Sue held Jelly Bean's leash in one hand and an animal crate in the other.

"Jelly Bean is staying with you today."

"He is?"

Jelly Bean blinked. He wore a blue collar studded with shiny blue stones, dazzling in the early morning sunlight.

Nettie Sue spoke in a monotone. "Candy said you were off work. Papa has to have some tests run at the clinic this morning. Jelly Bean's not allowed. He likes you. I couldn't leave him with anyone else."

Was she supposed to be flattered? "How do I take care of him?"

Nettie Sue squeezed her brows together and gave her a strange look. One that said *doesn't everyone know how to care for a pig?*

"He's already had his breakfast. So, don't worry about feeding him. He does like apples, though." She set the kennel in front of Annie. "His bed makes him feel secure."

"How long will you be? I have to leave for an out-of-town appointment by ten o'clock this morning, and I have errands to run."

"I'll pick him up by ten. Jelly Bean loves to ride in the car. Just put him in his kennel where he can see out the

69

window. If he needs to go outside, he'll nudge you on the ankle."

She handed Annie the leash. "He's also good protection. I hear you need it." With that, Nettie Sue turned, went to her truck, and drove off.

Protection? From a pig who couldn't stand to be left alone? "Well, Jelly Bean, it looks like it's you and me."

Jelly Bean grunted and nuzzled Annie's pink scruffy slippers.

With directions to the store for manure and pine straw and Jelly Bean in his crate at her side, Annie headed to Redfern Farms with the windows down. Jelly Bean raised his head, whiffing the air.

"You like the smell of the pine forest, buddy?"

Jelly Bean made a soft grunt.

"Me too."

At the farm, fenced pastures of grazing horses led to a red barn with paved parking.

She pulled into a shady spot alongside a couple of trucks, one green and one blue. Both had red bumper stickers advertising the farm's horseback riding.

"Jelly Bean, those bumper stickers look like the one on the truck that ran me off the road."

Jelly Bean twitched an ear.

"Stay here. I'll be right back."

Inside, the barn, she ordered the pine straw and manure from a tall, sinewy man with hair slicked back in a ponytail. His name badge identified him as Sandy.

"My mom assigned me upkeep on her rose garden while my parents are out of town."

"Our manure is cured and good for roses. Won't burn the flowers." He turned and spoke to the men behind him. "Bubba, grab two bales of straw. J.W., load a couple bags of manure on a hand truck and bring it to me." The men did as directed.

"Lead the way," Sandy said. "We'll load your order."

Bubba and Sandy followed behind Annie. She opened the hatchback and Bubba loaded the straw. Jelly Bean shifted in the kennel, poked his snout out and sniffed.

"What are you doing with the Forehand's pig?" Bubba asked in a manner suggesting she might be guilty of pig theft.

"Pig-sitting for Nettie Sue. You know Jelly Bean?"

Sandy loaded the manure sacks. "If you live in Sweet County, you know that pig."

Annie pointed to the truck bumpers next to her car, "Those bumper stickers, are they just for employees?"

"No. We had a box full. Gave 'em to workers and customers. If you want one, I think we're out. Bubba, we got any of those stickers left?"

Bubba shrugged and headed back to the barn.

"That's okay," Annie said. "But if you find one, would you save it for me?"

"Sure." He closed the hatchback.

"I'll leave my name and number in case you do." Annie took out her purse calendar and flipped past the auto body name Al Redfern had recommended to get to a blank page. She jotted down her information and handed it to Sandy. "Do you know Bud Dillman?"

"Yeah. He lives up the road a ways."

"I understand he does auto body work."

"Sometimes."

"Could you give me directions? I'd like to have him look at the damage done to my car when I was run off the road."

Sandy walked to the side of her car. "Ol' Bud could probably handle that." He gave her driving directions. "Dillman's mailbox is shaped like a tractor."

"Got it. Thank you."

Annie climbed in her car. "Ready?"

Jelly Bean laid sphinxlike on his cushion-lined cage, front hooves extended.

Driving away, Annie glanced in her rearview mirror. Sandy leaned against the hand truck, his arm draped over the handle. Bubba observed from the barn entry. Her departure apparently captivated them.

On Screech Hollow Road, Annie had no trouble spotting Dillman's unique mailbox made from the front of an old tractor. You apparently had to lift the hood to get the mail. She pulled into the driveway, put her car in park, and opened the door.

A pit bull charged from nowhere, barking and slobbering. She pulled her foot inside and slammed the car door shut. Thankfully, the dog reached the end of a heavy chain. Jelly Bean stood and pushed up on his hind legs to peer over the dash. The dog continued to bark and drool.

"Jelly Bean, stay down. We don't need to give him any dinner ideas."

Annie beeped the horn, sending the dog into an accelerated barking frenzy.

A burly man with a chest that matched the dog's came out of the barn wiping his hands on a rag. "Tank, quiet." The man approached her car.

Annie cracked her window. "Are you Bud Dillman?"

"Yeah."

"I'm Annie McAfee. I was told you do auto body work. Could you look at my car and give me an estimate?"

He saw Jelly Bean and frowned. "What are you doing with the Forehand pig?" A wary mistrust settled on the hard line of his jaw.

"Nettie Sue asked me to watch him." Actually, Nettie Sue told Annie she was keeping him, but she didn't think this guy would appreciate the distinction.

He scowled, but his jaw muscle relaxed noticeably.

"Show me your damage."

"Uh ... it's on the passenger side. Can I—"

"You can get out when I'm here."

Annie eased her car door open, watching Tank. He lay his head on his front paws, feigning sweetness. She followed Bud around the car and pointed to the damaged areas.

He felt the depth of the scratch and examined the dent. "I'd say you're looking at somewhere around a thousand in damages."

Annie's heart lifted a bit. Anything under the fifteen-hundred deductible would help.

He dusted his hands together. "Let me know if you want me to fix it. I'll have to order the paint."

"No rush. I have to save the money first. Have you repaired a white truck with damage on the driver's side?"

"Not lately."

"How about a gray or silver SUV truck with damage to the front?"

He gave her a steely stare. "Are you some sort of detective? You want your car fixed or to ask questions?"

Tank growled.

Annie took a step back. "A white truck ... forced me off the road. That's how my car was damaged. I just thought ... I mean if someone brought in a truck—"

"What I work on is between me and my customer. That new sheriff called me, asking questions. I don't appreciate being hassled."

"Sorry. I'll be in touch if I decide on the repairs."

Annie circled the rear of her car as far from Tank as possible. She cranked the car, backed out of the drive, and just like Sandy and Bubba at the Redfern Farms, Bud and Tank stood their ground, watching her depart.

CHAPTER 7

Will exited the elevator outside the governor's office. He spotted a man with a swath of salt and pepper hair hanging casually across his forehead, friendly yet businesslike. He fit Will's idea of what Craig Dillavey should look like.

The man approached. "Will Brice?"

Will nodded. The man extended his hand. "Craig Dillavey. Thank you for your punctuality." Making a sweeping gesture, he ushered Will into the governor's suite.

All night long, Will had vacillated between staying in Sweet County or resigning. The barber shop trio this morning capped it for him. He'd resign, go back to the state agent job he'd worked hard to attain, and do whatever was necessary about the accreditation issue.

If he was stuck in Sweet County, he couldn't prove his worth as a state investigator. Time to bow out and let the governor select someone more suitable to the area. He would not let them dissuade him. It wasn't like he was a quitter. He'd stay until they found someone to replace him.

Dillavey walked beside Will and paused at the reception desk. "Myrna, will you let the governor know we're here?"

"No need." The secretary, with short black hair and dark eyes that looked as though they could quickly size up visitors and their motives, exhibited a good-natured smile. "You must be Sheriff Brice. Welcome. The governor asked me to send you in when you arrived."

No waiting. A positive to contrast with the negatives Will had compiled since the governor's decision to appoint him as sheriff.

He followed Dillavey into a long rectangular room with a conference table at one end. The governor sat behind a large desk at the other end of the room. Behind him, the Great Seal of the State of Florida highlighted the wall flanked by the American and State of Florida flags.

Governor Renfroe stood and walked around his desk, offering his hand and a warm pat on the shoulder. He appeared as he did in his television ads. Good posture, pleasant smile with laugh crinkles about his eyes. "Mr. Brice, you've no idea what a pleasure it is to meet you."

Will took his hand. "Call me Will, please."

"Ray Goutter spoke highly of you, although he said it was unfortunate he didn't get to know you better."

Another man joined them. "Will, meet Philip Shashy, FDLE supervisor in charge of investigations and field operations in the Tallahassee region. Please, everyone, have a seat."

The governor returned to his desk chair. "Officer Goutter shared some information about the scarcity of supplies and equipment in Sweet County before he was taken ill. But, Will, I'd like to hear from you."

Will wasted no time on extraneous pleasantries and went straight to the facts. "Not only are we without supplies and equipment, but when Sheriff Daly left, his entire staff left with him. The Chief of Police was kind enough to temporarily loan me his part-time radio operator and some incident forms. I had to borrow walkie talkies belonging to the fair manager to work the local Confection Fair over the weekend. I can't access the locked file cabinets. The only keys left behind were for the two sheriff's office vehicles, and one of those cars was left on empty.

"I've had to scrounge for help willing to work for an unknown amount of time and pay. I'm currently operating with a skeleton crew of one patrol officer, one retired policeman on the radio who helps with patrol and his wife who assists with phones, buys food, and cooks for the jail.

"Some locals have already made it clear the town doesn't cotton to outsiders and pointed out that in past years, two appointed sheriffs met their demise under suspicious circumstances."

The governor raised his brows and eyed Philip Shashy as though they knew something Will didn't. Then Governor Renfroe leaned forward, arms folded on his desk, and spoke.

"I am impressed with how you have jumped in and taken over for Ray. You've entered a dry county where many of those who were supposed to uphold the law have allowed the illegal sale of alcohol for years. Some of the alcohol comes from moonshiners in clandestine operations. But much of the whiskey is illegally imported from outside sources. This practice has handed drug dealers a readymade pipeline to hook into. Of course, the influx of dangerous drugs is statewide, but Sweet County is unique. When I ran for this office, I pledged to clean up illegal practices across the state. Bottom line, no way do we want to see you fail. Here is what we've done and will do for you.

"Craig has contacted the head of the county commission to release budgeted funds. I spoke to Sheriff Daly regarding missing equipment, and he is cooperating. He assures me he wants no more conflict with the state attorney. Supervisor Shashy has arranged for three agents to come for a few days to assist you with administrative needs."

Shashy nodded his agreement, and the governor asked, "Philip, do you want to fill in Will on your undercover agent?"

"Certainly." Shashy turned toward Will. "We are fortunate to have an undercover agent already in place in Sweet County who is smart, quick with spur-of-the-moment thinking, and saved the day for another agent who got burned during a drug buy. Under the code name Mary Hart, she's worked in various roles behind the scenes and proven to be very believable in different scenarios."

The governor's intercom buzzed. He responded, "Go ahead."

"Agent Hart is here."

"Send her in."

Before Will turned around, the woman breezed by, leaving a trail of familiar lavender scent. She sat down with an air of confidence beside the FDLE supervisor. There was no indication she or anyone else noticed his gaping mouth.

Mary Hart looked exactly like Annie McAfee.

Because she was Annie McAfee.

Will felt like the spouse who is the last one to learn his mate has been unfaithful. She was believable all right. He believed her when she said she had no idea why anyone would target her. Why didn't she tell him she was an agent?

No wonder she knew to protect fingerprints on the cash and note she'd received and had her fingerprints already on file. To think he'd sympathized with the defenseless girl who had raised her bandaged right hand to swear she did not know why someone might want to harm her. News flash! She might not be as undercover as everyone thinks.

Supervisor Shashy continued. "Agent Hart, aka Annie McAfee, her given name, has the perfect cover in Sweet County because her parents just moved there and asked her to house sit. She has taken a summer waitressing job in a downtown café where she'll be privy to talk by the locals. Annie, share the information you've gleaned."

"Yes, sir. I've only been in town a short time, but I've seen an odd mix of attitudes. Most people are against wrongdoing. And yet they bury their heads in the sand when it comes to under the table alcohol sales because it's the established way of doing things. Paramedics told me that illegal sales come from back door operations referred to as unhinged."

She crooked her index fingers, denoting quotation marks.

"Unhinged because there is so much activity the doors almost fall off their hinges. Regular citizens distribute alcohol and likely other drugs, not dealers on street corners or back alleys. Statistically, Sweet County numbers for drug use and overdoses are low. But the county only has a small health clinic and no hospital, so serious cases are handled elsewhere."

Will glanced at the bandage covering the stitches on her arm. She didn't mention her firsthand knowledge of the small clinic.

"Drew, a paramedic I talked to at the café, said one facility reported incidents related to fentanyl usage has increased 700% in the area since the beginning of the year."

Governor Renfroe patted his steepled hands together and turned to Will. "As you can see, having an agent working to gather information incognito within your tight-knit community will be invaluable. Now, are you ready for your swearing in?"

How did this happen? He'd not said the first word about resigning, working until the governor found a new appointee, or his desire to return to his state agent post.

The governor had been warm, sincere, and disarming. He'd gone to great lengths to offer assistance. Will's gripes seem trite and selfish. Dillavey's statement the night he informed Will of the appointment—the only way you'll fail is if you turn down the job—hung like an anvil around Will's neck.

Will took the oath to perform the duties of the Office of Sheriff of Sweet County. After receiving congratulations and contact information for follow-up, Phillip Shashy excused himself. Craig Dillavey reminded the governor of a luncheon meeting.

"Any further questions for me before I leave?" Governor Renfroe asked Will.

"No, sir."

But he had several for Mary Hart.

CHAPTER 8

Annie waited for Will to speak when they reached the terrace outside the capitol building. Puffy white clouds rested on a backdrop of clear blue sky. The exact opposite of the thunderheads Annie perceived brewing inside Will. Only the sharp tweets of a bird and the distant honk of a car horn penetrated the nerve-racking silence.

Will stopped abruptly in front of the Officer Down statue, depicting a female officer cradling the head of a downed male law enforcement officer. Finally, out of earshot of others touring in the courtyard, Will spoke. "Why didn't you tell me who you are?"

"I was told to tell no one in Sweet County my confidential identity but Goutter."

Will's jaw visibly rippled. "I replaced Goutter."

"Precisely. And tell me that didn't make me worry. You could have been a plant and done something nefarious to get Goutter out of the way."

"You seriously think the person the governor appointed is not to be trusted?"

His words stung like a hard-hitting rain. "I did what I did because I thought it best under the circumstances. I'm in Sugarville for the summer, regardless. I need to remain in character and not react as a person who is working undercover. That is my job."

Will raised his eyes to the heavens.

"So, you're not a PR major?"

"Public Relations is my major. My minor is Criminal Justice. I do special assignment work for FDLE. I really interviewed for the PR job in the governor's office the other day. Perfect cover."

"And also the perfect way to raise suspicion."

"I can't control what people think."

Will turned his focus from her to the statue. A wall of tension smoldered between them while Annie absorbed the inscription on the memorial.

[Wording on statue block starts]

To past, current, and future law enforcement officers, our hope is that this Officer Down Memorial will be an inspiration and reminder of the courage, honor, and sacrifice which go with the calling of being a law enforcement officer.

[Statue block ends]

The words niggled Annie's sense of gratification in playing a role in law enforcement.

Will finally spoke. "The message on this plaque and the oath I just made as sheriff embodies what it means to be a law enforcement officer. I asked you to level with me and tell me if there was any reason someone was targeting you."

He spoke with sincerity, but Annie was no less earnest. She'd handled the situation the way she thought best at the time. "I know. And, if you recall, I didn't say there was no reason."

"You raised your right hand and shook your head. What was I supposed to infer? You even pretended to be an amateur on the police radio when you saw the fix I was in."

"I've never operated a police radio. And I was undercover. I wasn't supposed to just pick up and know how to handle the radio."

Will puffed out his cheeks. A couple approached the statue. Will touched her elbow and steered her over to the Florida Sheriff's Association granite wall of fallen heroes.

"Do you remember when I said you had the worst luck of anyone I'd ever met?"

"Yes." She touched the stitches on her arm.

"I take that back. The worst luck title belongs to me."

"Are you implying I'm bad luck?"

"No. I'm making a statement of fact. What I want now is for us to be on the same page. For me, the task is to discover what laws are being violated and to uncover illegal trafficking coming into the county while conducting the business of the sheriff's office. If you are playing newcomer and waitress in town, then I need you to stay out of the way, keep your ears open and mouth closed unless we are in a safe place to talk. I can't do what the governor wants if I'm running around trying to save you. It's obvious there is a crack in your cover."

"Obvious? I've done nothing that could make anyone think I work for the law. My being an agent surprised you. I saw it written on your face."

He halted and held up both hands in surrender. More people were milling about the courtyard.

He pinned on a cordial smile moved to the center of the courtyard. "Where did you park?"

"Kleman Plaza to the right."

"Figures. I'm in the lot on the left."

Figures? How had things gotten so off track? "What is that supposed to mean?"

"Just that we seem to tug in opposite directions and shouldn't. I'm sorry to be ... sorry. I just don't like surprises. And that is even a sorry excuse. We have to work together."

"Of course. I knew I'd be able to explain my position eventually, but ... being undercover..." She lifted her shoulders in I-hope-you-understand fashion.

He pressed his lips together, the gesture more impatient than understanding.

"You may not control what people think or surmise, but you can control what you do. Keep that in mind."

His words scraped over her like sandpaper. "I will."

"Being undercover, you will need to continue in your role, and we'll communicate as friends, which is a natural outgrowth of working your case. Agreed?"

Wasn't that what she'd already been doing? Was he just wanting to be in charge? She could play his game. She'd make him amazed at how well she controlled appearances. She plastered a smile on her face and held out her hand, still sore but healing. "Agreed."

Will flexed his hands around the steering wheel of the state car in the parking garage. He'd been so caught off guard, he'd forgotten to ask what he should do with the state vehicle. Tugging on his tie knot, he loosened his collar. He'd been welcomed and assured assistance by the governor. Why was he so upset?

Face it. The situation blindsided and embarrassed him. Annie emerged from her undercover cocoon as confident Mary Hart, breezing in like a lovely butterfly to present all she'd discovered in a short time on assignment.

He had been concerned, sympathetic—even attracted to this vulnerable woman who needed protecting. But she didn't need protecting. She was a special agent and one who had impressed her superiors.

Will had only complained and talked about needs. A whiner. She'd put him in a position where he couldn't quit. How would that look to the governor and FDLE?

Being left out of the loop made him look and feel foolish. He had suspected something more was going on with Annie and had asked about a reason someone would target her. She lied. He believed her. Stupid.

And the clincher? He had thought himself special to be accepted as a state agent. To learn Annie was an agent and had been working undercover for a year jarred him. He hated to admit it, but he was not only shocked but envious. Didn't his Sunday school teacher say something about envy rotting the bones?

He'd planned to resign and go back to FDLE to work out the certification issue. Annie thwarted that strategy when she stepped into the room. How could he possibly resign with the regional director standing there? He'd be deemed a quitter. Who would want to work with him?

And worst of all, Annie was right. She should stay in character to achieve the desired results.

He snorted. "So, you're jealous, resentful, and embarrassed."

Righting wrongs, helping to uncover crime, bringing bad guys to justice—wasn't that what he'd trained for? Hadn't he learned there would be bumps in the road? Problems to overcome?

Yes. Yes. Yes—the answers to all his questions. He bumped the heel of his hand on the steering wheel. He'd stay and perform his duties as sheriff. When the on-loan agents arrived, he'd discuss what to do with the state car.

He huffed, cranked the car and, pulling from the parking garage, headed back to Sweet County.

CHAPTER 9

Annie lifted the last bundle of Redfern pine straw out of the wheelbarrow and spread it over the manure she had watered in around the roses. The rose-tending project and forty-five-minute drive from Tallahassee had given her time to mull over the confrontation with Will.

You seriously think the person the governor appointed is not to be trusted? Will's question pricked just like the thorny rose bushes. She hated upsetting him.

Will duplicated the same perplexed look she'd grown accustomed to seeing on her father's face over the years.

"Evelyn," he'd said to her mother, "Annie is a mess. God must have blessed us with her to teach me patience."

"But, Jim," her mother had retorted. "She means well."

Then Dad drove home his point. "Eve meant well went she shared the fruit with Adam."

"He didn't have to eat it," her mother reminded.

"Ah, the lessons of the Bible are never ending," her dad concluded.

Though she afforded her parents many dilemmas to reflect upon, Scripture always settled the predicaments.

Will might be leery of working with her and not ready to view her as an asset. But facts were facts. She had training plus experience in her corner. She'd work to earn his trust, but she, like Will, had a job to do.

The mailman pulled up to the mailbox. She scrubbed at the perspiration on her forehead with the back of her gloved hand and trotted to the end of the drive where the lion statues stood guard.

"Hi, Mr. Letterman. I think that is the coolest name for a mailman."

"I get comments like that all along." He flicked up the bill of his postman cap. "I guess delivering mail was in the cards for me at birth. Sure is nice to be delivering to this house again. It stayed vacant about four years after Mr. Fleming died. When he lived there, he rarely showed himself. Strange man—just him and his cat, I understand."

"Did you ever hear the house was haunted?"

Mr. Letterman's eyes clouded. "Some say Mr. Fleming may have left in body but not spirit. Word circulated the church should send in ghost busters before closing the deal." He opened the mailbox and tsked. "Somebody put a card in your box."

"A card? Maybe an invitation?"

"People don't realize you aren't supposed to put anything in a mailbox that isn't officially stamped mail."

Annie peered into the box and took out the small envelope.

"Here's the rest of your mail."

"Thanks." Annie accepted the stack from Mr. Letterman and waved as he pulled away. She held the mysterious envelope up to the light. There were no marks on the outside and the flap was tucked not sealed. Putting her gloves back on, she carefully opened the envelope. On one side of a notecard, cut out letters that appeared to be clipped from a newspaper formed a message.

GO TO THIS HUNTING CABIN TONIGHT, AND YOU WILL FIND THE TRUCK YOU'VE BEEN LOOKING FOR.

A simple map was drawn on the back of the card.

Annie returned to the house. Peeling off her sun hat, she tossed it on a chair and placed the note on the kitchen counter. After transcribing the information to a separate sheet of paper, she placed the card and envelope in a paper sack to give to Will. Either someone was trying to help her anonymously or trying to set her up for an ambush.

After she worked the dinner shift at Candy's, she'd contact Will to go with her. Maybe she could make amends along the way.

The courthouse clock chimed one o'clock when Will reached Sugarville's town square. An eerie, ghostlike quality hovered around the stores with closed signs in the windows. A cat, prancing along the sidewalk as if sightseeing, produced the only activity. Will wasn't sure if the cronies at the barber shop were kidding about the appointed sheriffs residing in the cemetery, but their assertion downtown shutdown on Monday afternoons was real.

Candy's, where Annie worked, was closed until 5:00 p.m. The last time he'd ridden by the closed café was on the historical tour, sitting next to what he believed to be an endangered Annie.

Who was she, really? Quirky and unpredictable or a clever performer? What he'd learned today strongly supported the latter. He had noted the cautionary measures she'd taken dealing with the threatening note and cash but had failed to delve further.

Rather than contemplating who she was, he should put the question to himself. Who was he? He didn't like being fooled by Annie, but he'd been comfortable sitting beside her on the carriage ride, which was unusual for him. Annie, aka Mary Hart, put him at ease, and because she did, she troubled him. He sucked in air to settle his senses and continued around the square. He'd better knuckle down and move forward with his reopened mission.

Bob's Barber Shop had a closed sign and another sign that read: *See you at the golf course.*

Will parked at the sheriff's office and went in.

"Pee Wee, any news?"

"Just a few calls asking if it was true the governor appointed you sheriff. How'd it go in Tallahassee?"

"Okay. The governor conferred the title of sheriff officially."

"Why the long face? You should be flattered to be selected."

"Flattened is more descriptive." He couldn't express the entire reason for feeling deflated after discovering Annie was an undercover agent. She had the job he'd drooled over for years, and she'd gone in right out of college, with no experience, and must have passed her probationary period with the glowing reports from superiors. Take depression and jealousy, stir in responsibility for a county named Sweet, and you make a not-so-appetizing, bittersweet jelly roll.

Will heaved a sigh. "The job is mine to handle or foul up."

"I've been around you long enough to know, if nothing else, you'll work tirelessly at whatever task is given. You'll do just fine."

Like a cool breeze on a hot day, Will drew on Pee Wee's confidence. Will had always worked long hours. Crime doesn't punch a time clock. His mother had taught him that an idle mind was the devil's workshop, and the lethal effect of an idling car in a closed space could confirm that lesson. No idling. Keep busy.

"If I get any flak to the contrary, I'll send them to you to set them straight?"

"You've got it."

"According to the scuttlebutt at the barber shop, most of the downtown merchants frequent the golf course on Monday afternoon. Since it's quiet here, I'll go relationship building."

"Good call. Tommy and I have you covered."

When Will landed the agent job with FDLE, he'd given up his apartment, since he'd be traveling, and put his belongings in storage. A friend had given him a set of used golf clubs for use "during down times." Those times had yet to materialize. The clubs, thus far, did nothing but take up space in his trunk. Time to try them out.

The hours posted at the golf shack fit the community. They were closed Monday mornings and open in the afternoon. Inside the shop, Will introduced himself to the clerk.

"Say. You're the new sheriff, right?"

"I am."

The man who wore round-rimmed glasses and a friendly smile came from behind the counter and clasped Will's hand. "Pleased to meet you. I'm Royce Tinsley. How are things going for you?"

What 'things' was he referring to? Things covered a broad spectrum. Animal. Vegetable. Mineral. Pick any one or all categories and he did not know how they were going at present. The governor sent him to stop the illegal import of alcohol and drugs that apparently had been protected and accepted in a town humming along just fine until outsiders stepped in and ruffled the water. Like a pesky wind rocking boats in a cozy harbor, his arrival on the scene stirred feelings not appreciated by all.

The warning on the billboard at the county line to enter at your own risk set the stage. Keep things as is or keep going. If that was the crux of Royce Tinsley's question, Will was here to make certain things weren't going well. But he doubted Royce desired an in-depth analysis of 'things,' and he was not inclined to unpack them for him. He was here to disrupt a town largely content in its current state.

"Adventuresome," Will finally said in answer to Royce's question. "The governor made the appointment official this morning. Right now, I'm trying to learn more about the community. The barber shop patrons told me I could meet people at the golf course on Monday afternoons."

"Yes, sir—a tradition in Sweet County. If you want to meet people, this is a good place to start. But the usual foursomes are already on the course."

"Not being much of a golfer myself, I'd be a drag to a foursome, anyhow." Will pointed to the photo of the course on the wall. "I see you have a pitching green by the putting green. Do you have buckets of balls for practice?"

"Our golf pro, Sidney Burnell, hasn't run the ball picker yet, so I won't have any buckets of balls for practice for about an hour."

"I'll buy a pack then."

"Sure thing." Royce placed a 12-pack on the counter. "That chipping green doesn't get much use because a water hazard is so close. That was something—the governor firing the sheriff. I hear the whole department went with him."

"You heard right."

"I haven't lived here long, but the governor's decision has gotten mixed reviews."

"How's that?"

"Some people tend to resent strangers coming in and telling them how things should run in the county. Their rationale is if you grow the corn or cane you should be able to make and distribute it in the way you want. It's a crazy paradox. People want dry county rules yet want the privilege to skirt around them. I'd hate to be in your shoes."

Will snickered. No more than he was hating it right now. "It's not a position I would have applied for, but I guess I'll have to make the best of it."

"How much for the balls?"

"We're out of our cheaper brands. Right now, all we carry is our pro line. $49.99 a dozen, $53.99 with tax."

A tightness hit Will's throat. Conferring with the head of the county commission about funds just jumped to the top of his to-do list. This new job of his was all outgo and no income so far. "That could buy me lunch for a week at the downtown café."

"These balls are expensive, but they will give you good lift."

"Lift to the poor house," Will said, reaching for his wallet. "Since I've come this far, I'll take a box and hope they last me."

Royce gave him a course map.

"Is there a way to park my car close to the range so I can hear my police radio?"

"Use the service road." Royce pointed on the map. "It runs real close to the practice green."

Following Royce's instructions, Will traveled to the service road, retrieved his golf bag from the trunk, and headed to the practice green.

Will retrieved a pitching wedge. His first swing at the ball dug into the grass and sent the ball all of two feet. A black bird soared overhead, took a seat on a pine limb next to the range, and cawed what sounded like "ha ha ha." Will's next swing sent the ball straight up about thirty feet in the air. On its descent, it hit and rolled—as if it had eyes—right into the water hazard.

In thirty minutes, Will sent every one of his four-and-a-half-dollar-balls-with-"good-lift" into the pond. He sucked in air and plunked his club back in his bag. The black bird squawked and swooped over the pond, following the same path his golf balls had flown.

No way was he leaving fifty-four dollars' worth of brand-new golf balls in the water. Will walked down the grassy slope to the pond. He sat down, removed his shoes and socks, and rolled up his pant legs.

He calculated the balls should all be in about the same area. Only one had strayed a bit before the annoying splash. "I think Royce sold me water-seeking golf balls," he muttered.

The water, the color of strong tea, was warm and the sandy bottom was soft. He felt around with his foot until his toe bumped into something hard. He pulled out a shiny white pro ball.

"There's one of my strays." He tossed it on the bank and continued his search, wading along the hazard edge.

"Hey. What do you think you're doing?"

Will turned to see a man pulling up on a golf cart.

"I'm getting my golf balls."

"You can't do that."

"Watch me." Will continued feeling about with his toes digging into the sand.

The man, dressed in a green golf shirt with a Sugarville Country Club logo, slid off the seat of the cart and took a stance at the water's edge. "It's against the rules." He pointed to Will's unmarked car. "And that service road is for employees only."

"I just paid over fifty dollars for these overpriced golf balls in your golf shop. I hit them once and intend to get my money's worth out of them."

The man planted his fists on his hips. "I'll call the law then."

Will tossed the ball he held in his hand on the bank and threw up his hands. "I am the law."

"What kind of law?"

Chagrined, but qualified to fit in with Sweet Countians who desired to skirt the law, Will waded out of the water wiping his wet hands against his trousers. "I'm Will Brice, the newly appointed sheriff. I heard at the barber shop the golf course is the place to be on Monday afternoons, but obviously my expertise is lacking. I just lost a dozen of your most expensive balls in the hazard." Will nodded at the pond.

The man's stern expression caved, and a smile lit up his face. "Well, Sheriff Brice, I guess we can give you an introductory break." He held out his hand.

Relieved, Will shook his hand. "Appreciate it."

"I'm Sidney Burnell, golf pro and glorified grounds keeper today. The course has been closed since Friday to encourage participation at the Confections Fair. Kids apparently used the course for a drinking party and left their trash behind." He nodded his head toward the garbage bag on the back of his cart.

Leaning down, he rolled up his pant legs. "Come on. I'll help you find those balls—on the condition you let me give you some lessons."

Will grinned. "That's a deal."

Sidney waded in the water where Will had been.

"Most of my golf balls hit where you are, but one strayed all the way on the other side. I'll go over there."

Will pushed aside lily pads and grassy growth on the opposite side of the pond and stepped into the warm water, feeling the soft sand squeeze between his toes.

Feeling around with his feet, something nudged his hand. A shoe. He grasped the shoe to move it out of the way, but it was heavy. He pushed the lily pads aside and saw why. The shoe was attached to a body, floating face down.

CHAPTER 10

The golf course had changed from rolling fairways and spacious greens to a crime scene.

Will had taken photos of the area, including evidence of a scuffle. There were shoe prints, trampled grass, upturned dirt. The broken reeds on the bank held a plug of chewing tobacco. He had sent for the FDLE crime scene unit and confiscated the trash picked up by the golf pro.

County Judge Hubert Wilkins, who also served as the coroner, squatted beside the victim, and puffed on a cigar.

"From the look of the boy, I'd say he's been dead a couple of days."

The deceased with a grayed face and bluish lips smelled of diarrhetic feces. A partially empty bottle of whiskey was stuffed in his pants.

Wilkins pulled another cigar from his pocket and offered it to Will. "Helps mask the odor."

"No thanks, your cigar is already providing good cover."

Wilkins grunted. "Looks like a drowning, but an unattended death requires an autopsy." He stood and adjusted his belt and shirt with buttons, straining to do their job.

"Does the county have anyone who handles autopsies?"

"No. We use the medical examiner's office in Tallahassee. They'll either send someone or ask for the body to be transported to the Tallahassee lab. Have your office call Meadows Funeral Home. They'll pick up the body."

Judge Wilkins shook his head as he peered down at the lifeless form. "A shame for such a young life to be snuffed out. He couldn't be more than twenty."

A sheriff's office car pulled in behind Will's car on the service road. Tommy strode over but stopped several feet back from the victim. He took off his hat in a respectful gesture and lowered his voice. "Someone called from the FDLE to inform you they're sending three employees to help out a few days and should arrive this evening."

"Good. They can handle administrative work while we concentrate on calls and this death investigation. Any missing persons reported?" Will asked.

"Yes, sir. I took a report from the Becks whose seventeen-year-old son, Adam, is missing. They just returned from an out-of-town trip and discovered the animals hadn't been taken care of over the weekend, and he wasn't in school today.

"They showed me a picture." Tommy grimaced and nodded toward the body. "Best I can tell, that's him."

"Call Meadows Funeral Home to pick up the body and notify the family to go there for identification."

"Yes, sir. Right away." Tommy hurried off.

Judge Wilkins wiped his perspiring forehead. "Sheriff, you look young yourself. Are you sure you're ready for this job?"

A fair question. He was young, but even though he'd served nine years in law enforcement, he was well aware he could always learn more. "No, sir. I'd never claim to be totally ready for anything, but I have worked several deaths. I will do all I can to find out what happened here."

Will waved off a dragonfly that lit on the boy's face. "Do you know the Becks?"

The judge harrumphed. "You heard of the Hatfields and McCoys?"

"Feuding families?"

"That's right. In Sweet County, the clashing clans are the Becks and the Redferns."

"Redfern. The one who has the horse carriage rides?"

"That's one of the bunch. Art has horses, and he has a twin brother, Al, who handles farm equipment."

"My deputy had to break up a fight between a Beck and a Redfern relative at the fair."

"Been feuding as long as I can remember, and I've lived here fifty years."

"What's the feud about?"

"Not sure. They seem to be born with a natural animosity toward one another. You put two of them together and you're guaranteed to have a fight on your hands. I don't envy you your job, sheriff." He puffed on the cigar, creating a cloud of noxious smoke. "No, sir. Don't envy you at all."

In the café kitchen, Annie added sugar to a large pot of hot tea and stirred to melt the sugar.

Candy peeked under the lid of a large pot, letting flavorful smells escape. "How was your Monday morning off?"

"Eventful. I picked up manure and pine straw and spread it in mother's rose garden and received a note in the mailbox."

She omitted the surprise she'd sprung on Will at the governor's office and his I've-been-betrayed-look. Like holding a hand of playing cards, she allowed only a specified few to see her hand. She shifted from her undercover persona into the parson's daughter, who would naturally solicit her employer's thoughts about the note she'd received.

"Note? An invitation?"

"Sort of. Look." Annie pulled the copy of the note from her pocket.

Candy examined the message and map. "Forget it."

"Why? All I want is a tag number."

"If this was legit, why not just give you the tag number?"

"Maybe they don't have eyes on the vehicle and just know where it can be found. I had hoped to save at least three thousand this summer. That won't happen if I'm out a bunch of money for car repairs."

Annie filled pitchers, some with sweet tea, some unsweet, and set them on a tray. "I think I should at least check out this lead. If you let me leave right at seven tonight, I'll still have an hour of daylight."

Candy gave her a skeptical look. "No wonder your mother asked me to look out for you. Linda Lynn can handle customers that come in after seven. You take that note to the sheriff, and—"

"Thanks. I will." Annie lifted a tray of water glasses and swished through the kitchen door, muffling Candy's "—let him handle it."

The evening dinner crowd buzzed with talk of a dead body discovered at the golf course.

"I heard Sidney Burrell found the corpse and notified the sheriff, who happened to be at the golf course."

"According to Bob Kittrell, the waiter at the clubhouse restaurant said there was a fight at the first hole and someone ended up dead."

"No. I heard the sheriff found the body, and the golf pro is considered a suspect."

Annie could only guess at the truth and would have to wait to hear the facts from Will. At seven sharp, she drove directly to the sheriff's office.

Deputy Singletree emerged from the front entrance and navigated between cars crowding the parking lot. The FDLE Crime Scene Unit truck occupied the curb space where her car had almost become toast.

She lowered her passenger window and waved to Tommy. He walked over, removed his Stetson, and leaned down to speak to her through the open window.

"Is this part of the death investigation?"

"You heard?"

"News flows like a gushing fire hydrant in this town."

"The crime scene specialists are wrapping up their work, and three agents from Tallahassee just arrived to help with administrative work. The sheriff is interviewing people last seen with the victim. I'm on the way to pick up another witness for questioning. Can I help you?"

Witnesses to interview, agents to utilize, and a death investigation to conduct. Serious stuff. She couldn't bother Will with her note. "No. You obviously have enough going on. I won't detain you."

He nodded and hurried to his patrol car.

Daylight would not last much longer. She'd tackle this task herself.

CHAPTER 11

Inside the sheriff's office, Will pushed back from his desk and pressed his lower back into his chair to relieve the tension. When he had returned to his office after speaking to the victim's parents, he'd jumped right into the country club investigation. While Will interviewed Adam's cousins, Larry and Hudson Beck, who had been at the golf course, the men sent to assist him from FDLE had begun gathering inventory from the former sheriff and his employees.

Speaking to the Beck cousins reinforced the sight of heavy sorrow he'd witnessed at Adam Beck's home after the parents had identified their son at the funeral home.

"Do you know where the bottle of whiskey found on Adam might have come from?" Will had asked his parents.

Mrs. Beck, seated beside her husband, jumped up. Her eyes shot accusatory daggers.

"I know where the whiskey came from. That Clint Redfern boy. And no telling what else he had. I guarantee you he had something to do with Adam's death, and he's going to pay." She raised a hand, her body quivered, then knees buckling, she tilted forward. Grabbing her beneath her arms, her husband steadied her, and she collapsed against his chest, sobbing.

Larry and Hudson had admitted to smoking pot and drinking moonshine they "found" under the high school bleachers. The cousins shared matching stories that Clint brought Jim Beam and weed brownies supposed to be a peace offering one of the Redferns sent with him. While waiting for Clint's parents to bring in their son for an interview, Will rewound the taped statement from Larry and listened so he could formulate questions he'd ask Clint.

Q. *What was the need for a peace offering?*

A. *Becks and Redferns clash. It's just the way it is around here.*

Q. *Considering the longtime family feud, do you think Clint believed the peace offering was sincere?*

A. *Clint's in love with Adam's sister, June. They are kind of like that Romeo and Juliet story. Clint would believe the moon could swap with the sun if he thought that would repair the hatred between the families. He's had to sneak around to see June.*

Q. *Did Adam resent Clint seeing his sister?*

A. *No. He helped cover for June. That night, Adam dropped her off at a friend's house for a sleepover, knowing she was going to sneak off and meet Clint in the woods by the golf course. Adam might have a big mouth, but he had a big heart too.*

Q. *What do you mean he had a big mouth?*

A. *Adam has always been a big, tough guy and likes to brag. The guy could bench a hundred-fifty-pounds. Played center on the football team. But he has a weak stomach and puked after a riding the Ferris wheel Friday night. We razzed him.*

He came to the golf course with an attitude. Like he had something to prove. He was embarrassed about getting sick and about our relatives getting arrested at the fair. He countered our teasing by showing how he could hold his liquor. When Clint brought the weed brownies, he scarfed them down. I didn't eat much. They tasted weird to me. It was as if Adam was ready to single-handedly buck the family tradition of hating the Redferns that has been imposed on us.

Q. Do you know how the feud started?

A. Some kind of water dispute over a hundred years ago. We play football together. We all agreed it's time the stupid feud ended.

His words trailed off in choked silence.

Pee Wee's voice on the intercom broke into Will's thoughts. "Mr. and Mrs. Redfern are here with their son."

"I'll be right out."

Will quickly listed the key questions he wanted to ask Clint. Outside his office, Will faced a slightly thinner Art Redfern look-alike. "I'm Sheriff Brice," Will said, hand outstretched. "You'd have trouble denying you're related to Art Redfern."

"Yes, my twin." With a stiff jerk of his head, Al Redfern introduced his wife, Frieda. Her eyes were red-rimmed, and she nervously wound a lace-trimmed handkerchief around her fingers. Clint, who stood a good three inches taller than Will's six feet, stepped up and introduced himself. Will ushered Clint into his office and closed the door, while his parents remained in the reception area.

"Clint, where did you get the whiskey you took to the gathering on the golf course?"

"From a box I found near the Moccasin Creek Bridge."

Unsurprised by another "found it" story, Will asked, "Was it left there for you?"

"No. I ... happened upon it. Some people buy it in Hill County and bring it over here. It must have fallen off somebody's truck."

"What about the weed brownies?"

He clasped his hands and stared at them. He'd apparently not considered how to explain them.

"Larry said they were a peace offering. Is that correct?"

"Yeah. Bubba, he works at the farm, knew we were having a get-together and suggested I bring them to share."

"Do you know where he got them?"

"I don't know. Made them, I guess."

"Tell me what happened at the golf course."

"We were talking about the fair and how Adam got sick after riding the Ferris wheel." Clint swallowed hard. "We were just goofing around, but I think Adam wanted to prove how he could hold his liquor."

"How much did he drink?"

"He had some shine Larry and Hudson brought—not sure how much. He bragged he was partial to Jim Beam and helped drain a pint bottle, started another, and ate a bunch of the weed brownies."

"Adam's favorite whiskey happened to be in this box you found?"

Clint nodded, averting eye contact.

"Then what happened?"

"I'd made arrangements to see my girlfriend and left."

"June Beck?"

He jerked his head up. "Yes, sir. Adam's sister."

"I didn't think Becks and Redferns mixed."

"No, sir. It's the reason we have to sneak around to see each other."

"What time did you meet?"

"Eight-thirty. We have this special tree ... in the woods, east of the green where I met the guys. We talked for a while, then she went back to her friend's house in case her parents checked on her."

"Okay. After June left, what happened?"

"When I went back to the green, Adam said Hudson and Larry had headed to the woods to take a leak, and he was going to see his girlfriend. Larry and Hudson came back complaining of stomach cramps. Then headlights appeared on the service road. We figured someone called the cops on us. Hudson and Larry ran to their car, and I ran to mine."

"What about Adam?"

"He had already started walking. His girlfriend's house is on the north side of the golf course."

"How was Adam when you last saw him?"

"Okay. He staggered a bit, but we were all kind of loopy."

Clint's sorrow-filled gaze met Will's. The heartbreak, like a scar, would always be with him.

After Clint left the sheriff's office with his parents, Will finished his notes, and stared out his office window. Clint Redfern and the other boys lied about the source of alcohol and marijuana. Now a young man was dead. And for what? Kicks? Bragging rights? The neon Sweet Dreams Motel sign popped on, glowing in hot pink.

Sweet dreams. After bedtime prayers, his mom had whispered "sweet dreams" to him. But her voice was stilled—different time, different place—in another pointless death. He squeezed his eyes closed and massaged his aching temples.

Lord, give me wisdom to ferret out the root of illegal activity in this town and stop anymore senseless death.

Will held the door to Candy's café open for the agents from Tallahassee. Tangy smells coming from inside made Will's stomach gurgle. After today's events, he wasn't sure what his body needed more—rest or food. But the agents needed to eat, and to be honest, the idea of seeing Annie enticed him more than he wanted to admit.

Candy cashed out a customer and popped the register drawer closed. Will held the door for the departing customer. A waitress, who wasn't Annie, cleared a table.

Candy greeted them. "Howdy, sheriff. Take the center table to give you plenty of room. Linda Lynn, bring everyone water."

"These men are here to help with the transition at the sheriff's office," Will said. "Introduce yourselves, will you? I'm so tired I'm doing good to remember my own name."

The men, Harry Rinse, Paxton Murry, and John Trent, obliged.

"Sheriff, I suppose you're plenty worn out, investigating the death of the Beck boy," Candy said, distributing menus.

Will gave her a weak smile. "Why am I not surprised you know about the investigation?"

"News in Sugarville spreads like butter on one of my hot biscuits."

The waitress brought water. While the other men talked about biscuits and food choices, Candy leaned in to speak to Will.

"Did you talk to Annie?"

"Was I supposed to?"

"Oh, boy." Wrinkles on Candy's forehead folded like a venetian blind. Deputy Singletree strode through the door as Candy grumbled. "Annie got a note, and she promised me she'd go to the sheriff's office and talk to you."

"I didn't see her." Will said.

"If you're talking about Annie," Tommy said, "she came by the sheriff's office earlier when I was leaving to pick up a subject. I asked if I could help her, and she said she could see you were busy and wouldn't bother you."

Candy's concern told him his workday was not over. "Candy, what was on the note?"

"Directions to a hunting cabin. It said to go there tonight, and she'd find who she is looking for."

A shot of adrenaline hit his system. Will stood, his chair scraping against the linoleum floor. "Do you remember the directions?"

"Sort of. You go out that county road, I don't know the number, but you turn by the blueberry farm."

"I know where the blueberry farm is."

"The note indicated going several miles until the pavement ends, then turning left on a dirt road. From there, it directed her to another road. I didn't get a good look at that detail. I know there are some hunting leases out there. One of them must have a cabin."

"Fellas, enjoy your dinner. Pee Wee has rooms reserved for you at the Sweet Dreams Motel behind the sheriff's office."

"You do what you have to do, sheriff," Paxton said. "We'll see you first thing in the morning."

"Tommy, I'll be on the radio. Have Candy fix you something to go. I want you on patrol if I call. I'm going by the parsonage first. If Annie was sensible, she went home."

But sensible didn't sound like a word to describe her.

CHAPTER 12

The remaining twilight had dimmed when Annie turned off the main road and inched her car along the dirt ruts. Dense woods of pine and underbrush lined the road, and shadows from the trees cast grayed images in front of her.

She glanced at her copy of the map on the front seat. Following this lead might be considered dangerous, but she was not immune to risk-taking since working on special assignment with FDLE. People offering anonymous tips was not unusual, and from what she'd learned from her briefing on Sweet County by her supervisor, the town's people had learned to accept a certain level of depravity for the good of the whole.

Being secretive about outing someone made sense, she reasoned, especially with a new sheriff in town. She'd worked remote assignments and stepped into uncertain situations on her own more than once. She'd handle this one by herself. Besides, she could place her hit-and-run case in the trivia column when compared to Will's death investigation. Why needlessly bother him?

The first nameless note writer had offered money for repairs and wanted her to not pursue the person who forced her off the road. But this writer offered to help her identify the culprit. To move this case along, checking out this lead was the expedient thing to do.

She came to two wooden posts matching those shown on the map. The heavy wire used to barricade the entry rested on the ground. Three trails branched off in different directions. As indicated on the map, she took the left road, drove a short distance and pulled to the side behind some bushes. She tugged on a black T-shirt to cover her white top and removed her .38 revolver from the glove compartment. Stepping from the car, she secured the holstered gun at her waist and patted her rear pocket, making sure she had her phone to take a picture of the truck and tag.

Locking the car, she slipped into the shadows while dogs howled and barked in the distance.

Will slapped his hand against his steering wheel when he saw Annie's car missing from the parsonage. But he had no time to waste on his frustration.

Following Candy's directions, Will reached the dirt road at the end of the pavement on County Road 2034 in fifteen minutes. He got out and examined the road for fresh tire tracks. If there were any, the matted grass on the rutted dirt road prevented tracks from showing up. He rolled down his windows and proceeded slowly, listening. The only sounds were the yelps of hounds a good distance away.

He continued past three locked cable entries—likely leading to hunting leases—when he spotted one with the cable down. Stopping, he scanned the area closely. Birds no longer chirped. Imprints of recent tire tracks were evident in the soft sand. The setting sun poked bits of orange rays through the trees. A glint of light further down the road to the left caught his eye.

He pulled the flashlight from under his seat and locked the car. Adjusting the service revolver at his waist, he followed the tire tracks, which led to a red Ford Fiesta— Annie's car—partially concealed in bushes.

His breathing shallow, he cautiously approached the car and shined the light inside. Empty. He tried the door handle. Locked. He shined his light next to the driver's door. There was no sign of a struggle outside or inside the car.

She was apparently on foot.

He made his way down the road. Keeping the flashlight beam at his feet, he checked for footprints. In the woods, darkness took over quickly. He detected the outline of a shoe print in a patch of soft sand. A print smaller than his.

To his right, the bushes stirred. He shined his flashlight toward the movement and black eyes stared back. A raccoon. Will's heart thumped hard in his chest. The same might be true for the coon.

Ahead, Will saw a shadowy figure. He turned off the flashlight and waited. The shadow moved forward. Crouching low to the ground, he moved ahead, taking cover behind trees. Each move countered by another.

The figure ahead moved again, then went down with a thud and a feminine grunt.

"Annie?" Will cast her name in a hoarse whisper.

Seconds ticked off, then came a soft, "Will?"

He hurried to her.

She remained on the ground and whispered. "How did you find me?"

"Candy."

"I didn't want her bothering you. You're in the middle of a death investigation."

"One is enough. I don't need another. You do know this was a stupid idea."

She raised from her prone position onto her elbows. "Not if I get the tag number I want."

"If the writer of your latest note was trying to help, why send you into the woods at night?" His hushed voice carried the sharp edge he fully intended.

She ignored his question. "There's a clearing ahead. I saw the outline of a cabin when I fell." She raised to a sitting position and pointed.

A *ka-pow* cracked through the dimly lit night.

"Get down. I believe your good Samaritan just shot at us."

CHAPTER 13

Ka-pow.

Another shot zinged, hitting the pine tree.

Will shielded Annie while shards of bark sprayed over them, stinging the flesh on her arms. He shoved her toward a large oak tree. "Take cover."

Annie's knees skated across protruding oak tree roots. Rough bark ripped her pant legs and underbrush bit at her heels. Rustling and crackling sounds came from the bushes near the cabin. The barks and yelps of dogs intensified.

For a few long seconds, the pulse hammering in her ears drowned any outside noise.

"Are you okay?" Will whispered.

Annie released the breath she held. She had scratches and hurt pride but answered, "Yes. You?" Her voice sounded tight and tinny to her own ears.

"Stay down."

"I can't take a picture if I stay down."

"Picture of what?" Will crouched beside her. "I'm more interested in dodging bullets than photography. There's no sign of a vehicle."

Suddenly, the area lit up behind them. Car lights bobbled, casting light into the trees, then shining low to the ground, moving along the bumpy road. The car, a Sweet County cruiser, screeched to a stop in the clearing.

Annie sneezed in the wake of the dust cloud kicked up from the police car.

Deputy Tommy Singletree stepped out. His headlights spotlighted the cabin and the fact that Will was right. There was no vehicle or sign of anyone to reveal who had run her off the road.

Stupid. Stupid. Stupid. She'd spent more time on the ground around Will than standing. Some agent she presented. She'd thought she was halfway good at her craft. At least her superiors had said so. Had she been overconfident? Let down her guard?

The voice of her finger-wagging father came to her. "Annie, when will you learn?"

The criminal justice program had offered no classes on taming spur-of-the-moment impulses. Her impulses had actually served her well and even earned her a bravery citation. But there'd be no accolades for her tonight.

Will stood, shielding his eyes from the glare of the headlights.

"I thought I heard shots, Sheriff."

"You did. How about turning down your brights?"

"Yes, sir." Tommy returned to the car and dimmed the lights. Annie pulled herself off the ground. Her shoulder throbbed as she tried to dust the dirt from her torn slacks. What a mess.

"Do you know where the shots came from?" Tommy asked.

"Not sure, but it sounded as though someone ran through those bushes to the left of the cabin after shots were fired."

"I heard rustling in the underbrush too." Annie said.

"Those dogs have treed something." Tommy said. "Could be coon hunters."

"Could the shots have been hunter's stray bullets?" Annie asked. The explanation worked for her and could take the edge off her ill-fated attempt at handling her own investigation.

"Not likely. Unless they didn't use common sense."

Will did not disguise the fact his words were meant for her as well. It was uncanny how Will emulated her father's curt assessment of her actions. She pinched her lips together. Now was not the time to plead her case.

"Bark flew from this tree." Will addressed Tommy, shining his flashlight on the pine tree. "You and I both know coon hunters would not shoot five feet off the ground."

Tommy pointed. "Right, and there's two holes close together."

Will took out his pocketknife and handed Annie his handkerchief. "Use this to hold the extracted bullets."

She opened the handkerchief and made no argument. Avoiding handling the bullets meant the possibility of capturing fingerprints. Tommy held the light while Will cut around the bullets and let them drop into the cloth. Annie carefully tied the corners of the handkerchief to hold the evidence and handed the bundle to Will.

"Secure the area, Tommy. I need to take her home."

"Oh, you don't have to—"

"Yes. I do." He gave each word special emphasis.

"Being shot at had to be pretty scary for you," Tommy said. "Best let the sheriff see you home safely."

Annie swallowed hard against her frustration with Will's attitude. She pulled her tucked shirt out to conceal her revolver. Her undercover role was to play herself as a waitress and house sitter with everyone, including Tommy.

"Fortunately, the crime scene specialists from Tallahassee working the golf course death left behind high intensity lights for our use," Will said to Tommy. "I'll retrieve them and return so we can scout the area for evidence."

Returning to her car, Will held the flashlight's beam on the road just ahead of them. He maintained a deafening silence, but a heat emanated from him.

At her car, she dug in her pocket for her key and pressed the button. At the sound of the unlock click, Will opened her door. She slid onto the driver's seat and placed her gun in the glove compartment, feeling like a scolded pup. "I know what you're thinking."

"Oh, I hope not."

"Okay, maybe not exactly, but I want you to know much of my work with FDLE has been based on sketchy information like this."

"And they sent you out to act on the information by yourself?"

"Well, no, but—"

He tapped on the roof of her car. "You lead. I'll follow."

Fifteen minutes later, she pulled past the proud lion statues onto the steep parsonage drive. Will stopped behind her. She set her brake. It would not do to roll into him and aggravate him further. Gathering her purse and gun. She started to open her door, but Will was already there.

Opening her door, he said, "Lock your car. I'm making sure you are in your house safely before I leave."

"Not necessary. I've put you to enough trouble, so—"

Will's stomach growled.

"—I bet you haven't eaten."

"Skipping a couple of meals won't hurt."

"Please. I know the deputy is waiting for you. Making a sandwich won't take long. It's the least I can do—"

Another gurgling sound came from Will's middle. "My stomach is telling me to accept your offer. And I actually would like to see the note you received. But I can't stay long."

Will held the screen door for her while she unlocked the front door.

Inside, Annie flipped on the lights. "The kitchen is straight ahead. A bathroom is on the right if you want to wash up. I certainly do." She started up the stairs that led to the bedrooms. "I'll meet you in the kitchen."

When Annie returned, Will was already in the kitchen, placing a call on his cell phone.

Annie took out sandwich makings while he talked on the phone.

"PeeWee, bring the high-intensity work lights to Sugar Street." He looked up. "What is this street number?"

"Eight one five."

He repeated the number, then added, "Call Chief Woodham. See if he knows who owns the property with hunting leases off County Road 2034."

Will settled onto a bar stool at the island counter. "Could I see the note you received?"

"I copied the message and put the note in a plastic bag."

Will smoothed the bag, viewing it through the clear plastic. His brow furrowed. "The cut-out letters alone should have been a clue this was not legit."

"I assumed they didn't want to be identified."

He shook his head. "You know what they say about assumptions."

"Yup. Number seven. We should not assume what others think, know, or want."

"Seven?"

"I numbered my dad's most often quoted lectures."

Her dad had afforded her lots of quotes to remember. About the time she was in first grade, she began to number them.

"What's number one?"

"An honest witness tells the truth, but a false witness tells lies."

"Too bad you didn't take it to heart."

"I understand that we shouldn't assume what others have in mind but why assume the worst? Why not assume the best and proceed with caution?"

"You call going by yourself in the dark to a spot you were directed to on an anonymous note made with cut out letters proceeding with caution?"

"I was trying to save you time. I had my gun."

"We see how well that worked out."

He paused and locked his gaze on hers. Annie wanted to plead her case, but it was riddled with holes—two to be exact.

"Look," he said. "Under normal circumstances, I'm sure you're capable of working alone. But these aren't normal circumstances." He tapped the note. "Didn't your law enforcement training teach you to use backups?"

"Yes, but we're also taught to move toward, not away from trouble."

"When others are in danger. That wasn't the case here. You drew gun fire."

"Aren't you making assumptions now? Why couldn't the shots have been strays from hunters?"

"If the perpetrator hit either of us tonight, he'd be glad to have the shooting declared an accident. But that theory would not stand up. Coon hunters follow their hound dogs. It's like a sport. The dogs trail the coon until it runs up in the top of a tree. Hunters shine lights high up to locate and shoot. The gunfire we encountered tonight was too low to be from coon hunters."

Will paused and studied both sides of the card left in Annie's mailbox.

Annie concentrated on unwrapping cheese from the wrappers but stopped short when Will spoke again.

"What we can surmise from tonight is the person who ran you off the road does not want to be discovered, and the shots fired were meant for you." He slipped the plastic-covered card into his front pocket.

Annie swallowed hard against the shock of his words.

"Do me a favor?" Will asked.

"Sure."

"Stick to your undercover role at the café, and let me work your case. I have enough on my plate without having to run after you."

His words stung. Her instructions were to work with the governor's appointee. Co-equal. Will wasn't to call all the shots. Prior assignments with FDLE allowed her to make independent decisions. "You were busy. I did the expedient thing by checking on the note myself." She sliced his sandwich with a flourish. "You didn't have to come after me." She stuffed the sandwich into a plastic bag and huffed out a quick breath. Confession time. "But I'm glad you did. I will confer with you on future matters." She slid the food in front of him.

"Good. And I appreciate the sandwich." Will stood, and a knock came on the front door.

"It's probably my deputy. Stay here."

Stay? A canine command? After she made a humbling admission that hurt like pulling a tooth?

Will touched the gun holstered at his side, checked the security hole, and then opened the front door.

The name Pee Wee suited the deputy standing on the front porch. The deputy's head barely reached the top of Will's shoulder.

"I have those lights for you and a situation to report."

"What situation?"

"On my way over here, I had to stop a couple of teens joy riding and hopped up on something. Do I lock 'em up or take 'em home?"

"Take them to the jail and call the parents. We'll keep them overnight."

"Two of the three holding cells are full. The two petty theft offenders couldn't make bond, and the plumbing is clogged in the third."

Pee Wee glanced at Annie and tried, unsuccessfully, to lower his voice to a whisper. "Boss, the prisoners stink. We made them shower, but they had to put their dirty clothes back on. We couldn't find any jail uniforms for them."

"Clean out a couple of cells upstairs. Hold the teens downstairs."

"Yes, sir. Oh, and Chief Woodham said Art Redfern owns several hundred acres off Highway 2034 and leases part of it to hunters."

One of the teens in the patrol car shouted, "McMichael, sing it like you mean it!" High pitched singing rose from the deputy's car. "I'd better go quiet them down," Pee Wee said.

"I'll be right there to help load the lights in my car, Pee Wee." He turned to Annie. "Promise me you'll stay inside and keep all your doors locked."

"No problem."

As Will trotted down the steps to the tune of less boisterous singing, the jail dilemma gave Annie an idea. She called after him.

"I'll be here working on something to help you out."

Will halted at the foot of the stairs, slipped her a please-no-more-favors look, then strode to his car.

CHAPTER 14

Will stared at the bedside clock until the red numbers came into focus. It was 5:00 a.m. He'd only managed to shut his body down for a couple hours of sleep after finishing the search in the woods where the shots were fired.

He plumped the lumpy Sweet Dreams pillow, turned his back to the clock, and hoped for a couple more hours of rest. Nothing doing. Clues continued to roll in Will's mind. He sat up, swung his legs off the bed, and lifted his shoulders to release the stiffness.

He'd worked late with Tommy, gathering evidence. They found and cast a shoe print and located gum wrappers and Kool cigarette stubs in a patch of pressed-down palmetto brush. Someone had evidently been lying in wait for Annie at the site of the shooting.

He might as well put his sleeplessness to good use. He snapped on the desk lamp and pulled the Gideon Bible from the drawer. Thumbing to Psalm 138, he read:

"... though I walk in the midst of trouble, thou will revive me ..."

"I could use reviving."

Since Will had arrived in Sweet County, he'd dealt with two hit-and-runs, one death, and been shot at. A boost to his soul was in order.

Will had inherited his father's stoic personality, but he also had his mother's tender heart with a love for God. The combination had led him to serve God through working for and protecting people.

But protecting Annie was a different story. She was so ... so ... What? Intriguing? Unpredictable? Likeable? She had revived his spirit after last night's scare. She was easy to talk to, and he admired her can-do attitude. Yet, her independence mixed with vulnerability frustrated him and could get her killed. Correction, could get *them* killed and then what good would either of them be?

No. The best label to describe Ms. Annie McAfee, aka Mary Hart, was exasperating. She must have some capabilities to warrant the praise of her FDLE superiors. He rubbed the scratchy stubble on his chin. Was he blind to her competence? He had to hand it to her. She was fearless.

But enough about Annie. He should make a list of administrative work for the men on loan from Tallahassee. He couldn't afford to waste manpower.

Inside the desk drawer, he found a Sweet Dreams notepad and began a list. Gather missing equipment—especially keys, record inventory located and compare to the state audit, list missing items, cover incoming calls, and free up Tommy and Pee Wee to go on patrol.

After compiling another list for himself, Will got ready and left the motel, entering the jail kitchen at 6:30 a.m. Bacon sizzled, and aromatic steam rose from the coffeepot.

"Good morning, Cheryl. You have it smelling mighty fine in here, but I thought you had radio duty."

"Agent Murry relieved me." She used tongs to turn the bacon. "He jumped at the chance when I offered to fix breakfast."

Will pulled a cup from a shelf and poured himself a cup of coffee. "Smart man. Have you seen the other agents?"

"Yup. After coffee, they moved outside to check VIN numbers on those old cars in the side lot. No grass growing under their feet."

"They're making me feel like a slacker."

"They know you were up half the night." She held up a piece of bacon and shoved a plate of biscuits toward him. "Eat."

Will munched on a slice of salty bacon and proceeded past the holding cells. The kitchen smells and sounds did little to cover stale booze odors and snoring coming from Pee Wee's rowdy teens.

At the front desk, Paxton Murry had his ear to the phone. When he saw Will, he covered the mouthpiece and said, "I put the former sheriff's keys that Harry and John picked up last night on your desk."

"Thank you for taking initiative after I ran out on you."

He shrugged. "You're stretched thin. That's why we're here."

A surge of renewed energy struck, and Will thought of the words of encouragement in Scripture he'd read earlier. "Maybe I can unlock the cabinets in my office."

He flipped on the office light. Three rings of keys held varying sizes of keys. He tried the smaller keys first. A lock clicked after several tries.

He fingered through the folders filled with old news releases, correspondence. The same key opened the other two cabinets. One held legal rulings, Florida statute information, and a fat folder filled with forms.

"At last," he muttered.

The third cabinet held case files dating back twenty years. In the bottom drawer was a separate section titled *Suspense Files*. What were suspense files?

The name Bruce McMichael caught his eye. He pulled the file and flipped through it. McMichael had been picked up for DUI two years earlier at age fifteen. Status—warning. Five months later, he was arrested for being drunk and disorderly at a high school football game. Status—Handed over to his parents, no charges made. Two months later, the teen was caught with a lid of marijuana. No charges. His father was called to pick him up.

He pressed the intercom button to reach Paxton. "Do you have the names of the teenagers picked up last night?"

"Yes, sir. Names are Harris Pomeroy and Bruce McMichael."

Will spotted another familiar name, Hudson Beck, who was one of the boys he'd interviewed in the death investigation. His file held two reports of intoxication and disorderly conduct. Again, parents handled the situation.

The files painted a troubling picture of Sweet County's lax practice of dealing with juveniles. Will pulled the entire stack of folders in the suspense section and plunked them on his desk. The intercom buzzed. "Sheriff, the coroner in Tallahassee is on the phone."

Will picked up.

"Sheriff Brice, I have the autopsy results on the unattended death of Adam Beck."

"What did you find?"

"The primary cause of death was drowning, but this boy had a blood alcohol level of 3.2, a toxic range for most." Will's swallow of coffee turned bitter, thinking of the tragedy. Boys meeting, drinking, and never thinking of the serious consequences.

"Any evidence of foul play?"

"Bruising under his chin. Could be from a punch or fall. But there's more. I found the remains of brownies laced with THC, fentanyl, and magnesium hydroxide in his stomach."

So, fentanyl had made its way to Sweet County. "What is magnesium hydroxide?"

"A laxative, which accounts for the victim's loose bowels."

Clint had mentioned that Hudson and Larry complained of stomach cramping. "So, the primary cause of death was the drowning, with alcohol and drugs a likely contributing factor—and we can't rule out foul play?"

"Correct."

After hanging up, Will closed his eyes and tapped his steepled fingertips to his forehead. The crime lab's forensic analysis of evidence gathered on the golf course would be even more essential in this case now. What locals had sloughed off and glossed over in suspense files had allowed drugs to infiltrate the town like sewage seeping into the county's water supply.

Illicit drugs usually meant some form of organized crime was involved. And organized crime bred shootings. Had Annie somehow posed a threat to the criminal element?

He placed a call to Art Redfern to find out the identity of the coon hunters on his leased property where last night's shooting occurred. Art wasted no time calling him back with the names. Will summoned Bubba Grimsley, Sandy Barnes, and Reggie Dillman to his office.

Within an hour, Reggie Dillman arrived, wearing an apprehensive expression. He removed his Ford insignia ball cap when he entered Will's office.

"I appreciate you coming in. Have a seat." Will took the usual demographic information. "I talked to your father a few days ago regarding auto body repairs."

"Yes, sir. My dad mentioned it. Is that what you wanted to talk about?"

"No, unless you have any further information about a damaged white truck or silver SUV."

"Uh ..." he looked at his boots, "no, sir."

"Where were you last night?"

"I met some buddies, Sandy Barnes and Bubba Grimsley on our huntin' lease."

According to Clint Redfern, Bubba was the name of the person who sent the laxative and drug laced brownie peace offering. "Is Bubba related to the Redferns?"

"Sort of. His stepmother's sister married Al Redfern."

"Why were you on the hunting lease last night?"

"We was just runnin' the dogs, you know, to see who has the best tracker—for braggin' rights."

"Did you fire any shots after dark?"

He looked up, concern etching his face. "No, sir. I thought I heard shots, but it wasn't any of us. We just wanted to tree a coon. We don't shoot 'em."

"Do you smoke?"

"My momma don't allow smokin'." He pressed his lips together with a slight grimace. "But I do chew a little now and then."

"Were all of you together the whole time?"

"Mostly. We might run into the woods some after our dog and be out of sight of the others. Not long though."

"Did you have firearms with you?"

"Just a .22 rifle on the gun rack in my truck."

"What about a 30-06?"

"I have one at home—my deer rifle. No need to have it with me on coon night. Especially since we don't shoot nothin'."

"Then you won't mind if I check your gun?"

He puffed his cheeks out, and his shoulders inched up. "No ... I guess not."

Bubba Grimsley came next. He was short, maybe 5'6", had a chubby belly, and looked the part of a good ol' boy. He offered a calloused hand to Will before sitting down.

Will wrote down his responses to the basics. His answers were straightforward—forty-eight years old, lives in ranch-hand quarters on Redfern Farms, has been employed there since he graduated from high school, drives a blue Ford pickup.

His story about the coon hunt matched Reggie's—no surprise. Will knew these guys would talk to each other and likely agree on what to say, but they couldn't prepare for the body language that often yielded more information than the words spoken.

"Do you own a 30-06?"

Bubba shifted in his seat, hooked one scuffed boot over the opposite knee and jiggled his foot. "No. Why would you ask me that?"

Defensive.

"Do you make brownies?"

He let his foot drop to the floor and clutched the belly roll at his waist. "I eat brownies. I don't make 'em."

Rude and combative.

After excusing him, Will made a few more notes about his impressions before calling in Sandy Barnes.

Sandy removed his cowboy hat and exposed long hair slicked back in a ponytail. He was tall and slender with sinewy, muscular arms. "Sheriff, good to meet you. You're a might younger than I would have thought. Maybe that's a good thing." He pumped Will's hand hard and hung on.

Will had to flex his fingers to get the feeling back after Sandy released his hand. "Why would being younger be a good thing?"

"Oh, you know. Can't teach an old dog new tricks and all. I bet being sheriff is pretty awesome."

"I don't know that awesome is the right word. Maybe just awed."

Sandy slapped his cowboy hat against his knee and barked out a chuckle that made the prominent Adam's apple on his neck bobble.

"Have a seat."

Sandy sat down and pushed back in the chair as if ready for a leisurely chat.

Over friendly.

After Sandy gave a similar account of the coon hunt, Will concluded the interview. "I appreciate your cooperation. Okay for my deputy to follow you and pick up your 30-06 for test firing?"

"Yes, sir. Anything I can do to help. Call on me anytime."

Will followed Sandy to his office doorway. At the same time, Annie walked in the main entrance, holding a large paper bag.

A smile of recognition crossed her face. "Hi. Sandy, right?"

"Right. Did you find your way to Dillman's yesterday?"

"Sure did."

"I found an extra bumper sticker. If you still want one, I'll set it aside for you."

"Yes. Thank you."

Bumper sticker? Dillman's?

Sandy left, and Will motioned Annie into his office and closed the door.

"When did you two meet?"

"Yesterday morning. My mom left instructions for me to pick up manure and pine straw from the Redfern farm for her rose garden. Sandy loaded the supplies and gave me directions to Dillman's so I could get an estimate on car repair. " She placed the bag on his desk. "For you," she said and took a seat.

Will sorted through the fragments of information he'd just taken in.

Did Annie's inquiries about the bumper sticker and going to see Dillman have any connection to last night's shooting? All three he had questioned were cooperative, yet edgy. Clearly, someone had been waiting for her in the woods. But for what reason? Undercover or not, Annie had a knack for complicating matters. And what, pray tell, did she have in the bag?

"I couldn't sleep last night and since I had a whole bolt of fabric left from the fair ..." Annie reached in the sack and let a pink item unfurl until it touched the floor. "I made two of these for you. Lessie finished the handwork this morning."

Will scratched his head. "Pink jumpsuits?"

"Jail uniforms."

Will clasped his hands beneath his chin. The lines between his brows deepened.

What did he think? Had she done something stupid?

"I was running on adrenaline after all that happened yesterday." She quickly folded the jumpsuit and stuffed it back in the bag. "A silly idea."

"I'm sorry. No, please. I appreciate your hard work." His weak smile turned into a wide grin. "Perfect for the guys upstairs who are waiting to be bonded out."

He took the bag to the front desk manned by Paxton. Annie peered around the open door.

"When Pee Wee wakes up, have him tell the smelly inmates upstairs to put on these uniforms. Cheryl can launder what they've been wearing."

Paxton grinned. "Will do, sheriff. Too bad you didn't have these for the two drunken teens brought in last night."

Will nodded and returned to his desk. Annie sat back down and let the breath she held ease out. Maybe her idea wasn't dumb after all.

"Are you always so productive when you can't sleep?"

Annie shrugged in resignation. "A blessing and a curse. I ripped up my dad's old coveralls and used them for a pattern. It's hard for me to be still and not do something, especially when I'm uptight. I've learned to channel the tension into something constructive."

"Well, thank you for directing your extra energy my way." Will's intercom buzzed. "Yes?"

"Call on line one from a Patrolman Newsome."

"Should I step out?" Annie asked.

Will shook his head, motioned for her to close the door, and took the call.

"Willard Fulton, 404 Honeysuckle Street, Sugarville, Florida. Claimed his boy was joyriding and hit a tree?" Will wrote while he spoke to the officer.

Will's auburn hair and ruddy complexion combined to make a nice-looking face, but his furrowed brow presented serious concern over the news he was receiving.

"Your paint samples from the Thornton's car matched? Jared Fulton. He admits to using drugs. Charges? I see. Thanks for calling."

He hung up and tossed his pen on top on the notes he'd taken. "Another young person making a bad decision and a parent trying to cover for him."

Will gestured to the stack of files on his desk. "These folders were grouped in a file cabinet under a suspense file label." Will selected a file and pushed it toward Annie.

Annie scooted her chair up closer and skimmed the paperwork inside the Jared Fulton file.

"Jared's first recorded infraction occurred when he was thirteen," Annie said. "The school bus driver called for a deputy when he couldn't wake the boy up to get off the bus. The father stated the boy was adjusting to prescribed medication."

Annie glanced at Will's sullen face. She pulled out the next report and recounted the details. "At fourteen, Jared was found incoherent, walking in the middle of the road, and taken home." She pulled out the last paper. "Three months ago, he ran his car into a ditch. A deputy called a wrecker to tow the car, per the father's request."

Annie closed the file. "Jared Fulton has a drinking and drug problem, and it appears he had no consequences or interventions."

"And now he's responsible for injuring the elderly couple on Old Water Tower Road." Will fanned out the files, exposing the tabs. "Suspense evidently means suspended action. Every one of the boys who had been drinking with

Adam Beck on the golf course have folders in the suspense section."

"Including Adam," Annie said, spotting a tab with his name.

"I received the autopsy results on Adam Beck earlier this morning. His death was due to drowning, but he had a toxic level of alcohol, plus cannabis, fentanyl, and a laxative in his system."

"Fentanyl is an insidious killer," Annie said. "I worked on a case in central Florida where we seized a huge shipment of cannabis laced with fentanyl ... on an anonymous tip." She couldn't resist the added remark and cut her eyes to Will.

He acknowledged her statement with a barely perceptible head nod. She'd best stay to the point. "But not before seven teens lost their lives and several others wound up in the hospital. Kids try stuff and may not be getting what they think. Like a laxative. That's a new one."

"The chemicals were found in weed brownies Adam ingested. The boys with Adam claim the brownies were supposed to be a peace offering from one of the Redfern clan to the Becks."

"Good gracious." Annie wilted in her chair. "We are dealing with feuding families, the tacit approval of parents covering their children's drinking or drug use, citizens who want to pretend no problems exist ... and all this in a dry county." She bopped her forehead with the heel of her hand. "I heard at the café that Mr. Thornton is still in the hospital."

"And Adam Beck is dead."

"Sheriff," Paxton called on the intercom. "Sorry to interrupt, but there's a news reporter here. He wants to know if you can speak to him."

"Give me a minute," Will answered.

"You want me to go?"

"No." Will gave the folders on his desk a long, hard look. "I'd rather you'd stay. We're going on the offensive."

He flipped the stack face down, concealing the names, and keyed the intercom. "Send him in."

A tall, thin man with shaggy black, chin-length hair and round, wire-rimmed glasses entered the office.

"Sheriff, thanks for seeing me on short notice. I'm Marvin Borg, folks call me Shag. I'm with the *Sugarville Weekly Journal* that comes out every Thursday." Words tumbled from him with the urgency of a man accustomed to having a door slammed in his face.

Will stood, shook hands, introduced Annie, and motioned for him to take a seat.

"I'll be dropping by weekly to check on incident reports, but first off, I'd like to do a story on you being our new sheriff." Shag pulled out a stenographer pad from his pocket and a pencil hidden in his hair.

"I grew up on a farm in Hill County. After high school, through the recommendation of a friend of a friend, I landed a job as a radio operator in Duval County."

"Moving from a small county to a county with a large population must have been a challenge."

"Twenty thousand to over nine hundred thousand. But the metro area allowed me the opportunity to take college classes at night and work up the ranks."

Annie admired his composure under sudden scrutiny. The way Will pursued his career spoke of a hardworking, self-made man.

"What do your parents think of your being appointed sheriff of the county bordering the place where you grew up?"

"My mother died when I was nine. She'd likely be proud. My father ... well, I can't speak for him."

Though Shag moved on to another subject, Will's hesitation made Annie want to know more.

"What do you hope to accomplish in Sweet County?"

"I've been sent to clean up graft in the county. I plan to enforce the law and serve the community until the citizens hold a special election and select a new sheriff."

"Do you have any additional information beyond the public record release about the body found at the golf course?"

"Nothing I can share right now, but I do have another news release."

Annie watched as Will glanced at the stack of files on his desk. Oh, boy ... what was he going to say?

Shag licked his lips and moistened the tip of his pencil with his tongue. "Go ahead."

"A sixteen-year-old juvenile, driving under the influence, was arrested for causing an accident resulting in injuries, property damage, and leaving the scene. The name must be withheld because of the defendant's age, but he will have to appear before the county judge in juvenile court."

"Who is liable in a case like this?"

"The parents, and they must appear with their child in court."

"Can I put that in the story?"

"Absolutely. Parents need to know the consequences of their children's actions fall on them until the child is eighteen."

Shag whistled. "That ought to make parents sit up and take note."

And make the crowd at Candy's buzz like flies on rotten fruit, Annie thought.

"To help inform the public, Annie has volunteered to put her public relations skills to work and develop educational material on the dangers of underage drinking and substance abuse."

"Wait. What?"

Will raised his brows and the barely discernible smirk on his face sent her the message this surprise announcement was his payback for the surprise she sprung on him at the governor's office. "Annie and I were just talking about helping young people make better decisions."

"Excellent," Shag said, turning toward her. "Okay to say you'll include information on wet and dry counties?"

She squinted at Will. "Sure, why not?"

Shag left. Annie vacillated between fuming and amusement at Will's audacity and craftiness. But before she constructed a reply, she was stopped by a clanging racket.

"Sheriff." Paxton's voice broke in on the intercom. "We have a disturbance."

"What's the trouble?"

"I believe it has to do with the pink uniforms Pee Wee took upstairs."

CHAPTER 15

"You're famous." Paxton strolled into Will's office, newspaper in hand. "You not only have prisoners who vow to never step foot in your jail again if they have to wear pink but listen to this write up."

He cleared his throat and read, "New Sweet County Sheriff set to sweep the county clean. Twenty-nine-year-old Will Brice is the new Sheriff of Sweet County appointed by Governor Renfroe. He states that—and this is in quotes—he's here to clean up the graft in Sweet County. He has been in some aspect of law enforcement since high school ... and there is more." Paxton held up the paper, letting the full front page unfurl. "Pretty impressive."

"Must have been a slow news week to put me as the headliner."

The phone sounded at the front desk. "I'm being paged." Paxton placed the paper on Will's desk. "All yours."

Paxton had read from the story about him, but the titles of three articles below the feature interested Will.

"Teen's Body Found on Golf Course," discussed the who, what, when, and where of discovering Adam's body and stated that autopsy results were pending. In "Sixteen-Year-Old Arrested in Hit and Run," Shag did an admirable job of sticking to the facts. But Will frowned at Shag's provocative heading—"Ready to Revisit the Wet/Dry Controversy?" The headline seemed aimed to stir the pot of public opinion. And maybe sell more newspapers?

The story read:

[News article block starts]

As a community service, Annie McAfee, daughter of the new pastor in town, plans to research and offer materials on the dangers of teen substance abuse. She anticipates raising the issue of wet vs. dry counties.

[News article ends]

Will may have blindsided Annie yesterday, announcing she'd develop substance abuse materials, but Shag bushwhacked him by twisting the subject to stir up opposing forces.

A light tap sounded on his office door. He saw no one, but called out, "Come in."

A black man, wearing a porkpie hat, cautiously stuck his head into the office. "Sir, the man out front said to knock. I hope I'm not disturbin' you."

"I'm off the phone. You're fine. Come in."

Stepping into his office, the short, bulky man with a large, round face pulled off his hat. "You being the new sheriff and all, I was hoping to catch you in."

Will stood behind his desk and reached to offer a handshake. "What can I help you with?"

The man took Will's hand and pumped it once with caution.

"Sheriff, I'm Rufus Tate. Could I talks to you man to man—I mean confidential like? You won't put me in jail?" He fingered the edge of his hat, rotating it along the brim.

"Not unless you've committed some big crime."

Rufus's eyes widened and bulged slightly from his eyelids. "How big?"

Will sat back down and motioned for the man to have a seat. "Like burglary, murder ..."

"What about bolita?"

"That's a game I'd like information on."

"You won't lock me up?"

"I haven't seen you do anything. No, I won't lock you up for information."

"Well, sir. I been doin' this bolita a long time. I had an agreement with the old sheriff. I pays him a little every week. He don't mess with my business, and I don't mess with his. I want to know what I need to pay to operate. I might raise what I was paying a bit if I need to."

Will folded his arms on his desk. "Rufus, I appreciate your honesty. As to how much it's going to cost you to operate, it may surprise you, but it won't cost you a dime."

Rufus pushed to the edge of his seat, taking a vise grip on his hat. "I don't think I understand."

"Let me put it this way. You don't pay me anything to run your business, but if I catch you, you're going to jail. Fair enough?"

Rufus stared. Then a slow grin upturned his mouth and spread to his protruding eyes. "Yes, sir. I gets you." He stood, smoothing the wrinkles from his hat. "Yes, sir. Fair enough."

He turned to leave, then turned back and dipped a slight bow before slipping his hat back on. "Nice meeting you, sheriff, but I hope you don't mind me saying, I hopes I don't see you again."

Will stood and shook his head. In spite of the man running an illegal gambling operation, he couldn't help liking Rufus. "No. I don't mind. But remember what I said."

"Yes, sir." He spoke the words with gusto and left, closing the door behind him.

The intercom buzzed. "Sheriff, you have someone else out here waiting to see you."

Will blew the stale air out of his lungs and clicked the button to answer. "Send them in."

The door opened, and a slim lady, fiftyish, with dark, gray-streaked hair pulled into a bun walked in. She stood tall and erect—a no nonsense, schoolmarm type. Thrusting the Sugarville weekly paper on his desk, she said, "Sheriff, I hope you are really here to do what you said in this paper."

"And you are?"

She made no apology for her abruptness. "I'm Nancy White. My husband is Ned White. He works at Sweet Used Cars on the highway. That is, if he hasn't lost the business playing poker."

Great. Just what he needed. A new issue. "Are you saying there is a high stakes poker game around here?"

"High stakes, low stakes, and in between. When somebody loses a week's paycheck, it might be low stakes to some, but it means my family has to live on peanut butter and crackers for a week. Last week, Ned lost the special-built barbeque grill we use for catering to supplement our income. The vice-president at the bank is cooking on it now."

"Who is involved in this game?"

"Mostly big wheels like that banker, and some who'd like to be a big wheel, like Ned."

"Do they play often?"

"Every Monday night. Sweet County Men's Club." She stood. "I'm off to shop for groceries. Best I stock my pantry before the next game. I'm telling you, if you mean to clean up the graft, start with that poker game."

Will stood and walked her to the door. "Thank you for coming in. I'll see what I can do."

She left in a rush. Will pressed his back against the wall and commented to Paxton. "What a morning. This place has more challenges than Olympic swimming. And I'm dog paddling in circles." Will heaved a heavy sigh. "I'll be in my office trying to keep my head above water."

"At least, it's quiet for now."

Will returned to his desk. Added to Annie's case and the death investigation, he had unhinged back doors, suspense files, bolita, and poker—revered customs to some.

What was he supposed to do? Become a daisy pusher with the two other sheriffs who dared challenge the Sweet County good ol' boys? Why him? He peered out the window with the view of an old, dented Pontiac in a patch of weeds and the Sweet Dreams Motel.

He didn't sign up for this. He closed his eyes, rubbing his temples with his fingers. Or did he? Maybe he had signed up as a youngster when he decided to become a lawman after his mother was killed. From his wallet, he pulled the photo of his mother, dead at age forty. She left behind a nine-year-old boy and a husband so stymied with emotions kept inside, he had nothing to spare for his son. Will was left to wallow in the hurt.

His salvation had been a track coach and a Sunday school teacher's policeman husband. From them, he received encouragement and motivation to move into a life of service.

He told Shag he was here to clean up the graft. Did he mean it? He glanced at the newspaper headlines again. His jaw ached, thinking of Adam Beck.

He meant what he said. He brushed his fingers lightly over his mother's photo. Her stilled heartbeat commanded him to serve and do what he could to remove corruption and obstacles that threatened people's safety.

He slid the photo of his mother back in his wallet, pulled out Investigator Sylvester Gaines' business card, and put in a call to the Escambia County Sheriff's Office.

"Gaines here."

"Are you ready for a special assignment?"

CHAPTER 16

Annie lifted the pan of lasagna from the oven. Jelly Bean raised his round snout and sniffed the rich aroma of cheese and meat sauce. "The sheriff is coming to dinner."

Jelly Bean blinked his pink lashes and twitched an ear.

Will had called, wanting to talk, and she'd offered dinner. Then Nettie Sue showed up with Jelly Bean, his pillow-lined kennel, a leash, and a large bag of chopped broccoli, Brussels sprouts, lettuce, and kale.

"Papa has an appointment in Pensacola, and I need you to keep Jelly Bean. I'll likely be late."

Jelly Bean had been at her side ever since.

She hoped to have a pleasant dinner, allowing Will a time to relax. He'd been under a lot of pressure since arriving in Sweet County.

The doorbell rang. Jelly Bean followed close at Annie's heels. She paused a moment to fluff her hair and check her makeup in the hall mirror. A peek through the security hole, then she opened the door to Will. He wore a fresh shirt and khakis, but the pallor on his face and low luster in his eyes suggested fatigue.

"Long day?"

"Am I that transparent?"

"Yes." She stepped back for him to enter. "Say hi to Jelly Bean."

Will squatted down to pet the pig's head and glanced up at Annie. "I think you can anticipate my next question."

"Nettie Sue had to take her father to an out-of-town doctor appointment and declared Jelly Bean was to stay with me. She did the same thing Monday."

"Presumptuous, wasn't she?"

"Out of all the people in this town, she entrusted him to me."

Will straightened. "Ah, you're honored to be selected?" A glint of amusement touched his eyes and warmed her heart.

Annie smirked and lifted her chin. "I like his company."

Jelly Bean looked from Will to Annie and back at Will, making a barely perceptible grunt.

"What's he saying?"

"He'll tolerate you." Annie nudged his arm and waved him inside. "After Shag's introduction of you in the newspaper, I believe the community will do the same. I received a call from Cora Neddles, the high school senior English teacher, asking me to speak about the dangers of drugs and alcohol because of the article in the newspaper. Adam Beck was in her class."

"Speaking directly to the students is a good idea. I've been contacted as a result of the news story too."

"Come to the kitchen and tell me about it."

"Something smells good."

"Lasagna, breadsticks, and salad. I hope you don't mind eating in the kitchen—the dining table is covered with a pink jumpsuit project on one end and substance abuse materials on the other."

"You're making another jumpsuit?"

"I have enough fabric to make three more."

"I shall not refuse your pink gifts. They should be patented and advertised as jail deterrents. And I'll eat wherever you say."

After dishing up plates, they ate while Will shared his news.

"The announcement I was here to clean up the graft drew out two more vices—bolita and high-stakes poker."

"What is bolita?"

"An illegal numbers game that has apparently been allowed to operate in the county for a fee." Will added air quotes.

"Does that tie in with the high-stakes gambling?"

"No. That information came from an upset whistleblower wife who is ready to shoot somebody over the poker game. Her husband just lost the special smoking grill they need for their catering business. I instructed Tommy to follow up on their game nights. My day has been an exposé of rats in their rat holes."

"I have the solution for catching rats. Rat jail."

"What's rat jail?"

"The kinder name is rat hotel. When a varmint goes for the bait, a trap door shuts him inside. I've been hearing noises in the basement at night. The mailman said the previous owner had a cat. With no cat, I'm thinking rats could feel emboldened, so I ordered the rat trap.

"Locking up varmints is a good strategy and one reason I wanted to talk to you tonight. I'm bringing in two beverage agents and an investigator from another county to work undercover."

"Did you talk to FDLE?"

"No. My directive comes from the governor. As sheriff, the buck stops with me. I took the evidence gathered from your case to the Tallahassee crime lab this afternoon, then met with the men I recruited. They'll each work a section of the county. They know how to blend in and make buys and will start work in a couple of days."

"No wonder you looked exhausted when you got here. So, if I'm working undercover, where does that leave me?"

"Following your FDLE orders to keep your eyes and ears open, which you apparently have done well in the past." He took a swallow of his tea, then set it down and asked, "What was the quick thinking your supervisor mentioned when you saved the day for an agent?"

"No big deal. I was a plant on a park bench listening remotely to a drug deal go down. A bad guy said, 'This guy is a cop.' I didn't like the sound of his voice and barged into the middle of the group, yelling, 'You're the guy. You took my dog.' I shoved him in the chest, and he dropped the gun he held on the agent. The agent grabbed the gun. And it was all over for the bad guys."

"That explains why your supervisor brags on Mary Hart. You are a woman of multiple talents. The way you operate reminds me of a computer running several different programs, one layered on top of another." He held up a fork with a bite of lasagna. "You're a good cook too."

"Thanks." Annie shrugged. "I thrive on activity, but I've not always received kudos for my creativity."

"No?"

"My mom made allowances for her eager daughter ... but not my dad."

Will reached for a breadstick. "Tell me more."

Was that a spark in his eye? Her goal was for him to have a pleasant evening. Unfortunately, chatting about her flaws seemed to do the trick. "Okay, so here's my sordid story." She took a deep breath and launched into her tale.

"In grade school, kids were sharing about what their fathers did for a living—like insurance salesman, store manager, computer tech. I told everyone my dad was a lion tamer, which was far more interesting than the boring stuff my classmates came up with."

Smiling, Will speared a chunk of cucumber in his salad. "Far more interesting."

"However, when the teacher invited my dad to share this profession in class, he made me stand in front of the room and tell them I lied."

"I'd have rather taken my chances in a lion cage. I prayed to melt into a puddle and disappear, but that didn't happen. I trudged to the front of the class and said, 'I lied. He doesn't tame lions, he just talks to a bunch of people once a week.' The teacher took over and explained that my father was a military chaplain."

Will's eyes twinkled. He said something she didn't catch because his smile highlighted an adorable cleft in his chin.

"Sorry, what?"

"I said, did you stick to the truth after having to confess?"

She adjusted the napkin in her lap. "I did, but I discovered telling the truth sometimes lands you into trouble too. At circle time when the boy next to me took his shoes off, I held my nose and hollered, 'Your feet stink, and that's no lie.' That episode earned me a lecture on propriety from my teacher *and* my dad."

From his laugh, Will clearly benefited from hearing her flubs.

"I believe that's when I started numbering the lectures. Before I forget," Annie reached in her pocket and pulled out a scrap of paper, "I saw a white truck across from Candy's this morning that looked like the one that ran me off the road, and I recorded the tag number."

"The last time you did that you ended up with stitches. Did anyone see you take down the number?"

"Well ... things were slow in the café, so I ran out and jotted it on a napkin."

"On the square, downtown, where anyone could see you?"

"I suppose."

Will turned instructive. "You are a waitress and a house sitter, not an investigator, and need to be viewed as such."

"A waitress on limited income would look for who messed up her car."

"Except the waitress was shot at and has been told to let the sheriff handle it."

"You sound like my displeased dad."

"At least *your* father showed emotion."

His mood shifted and took on a more serious tone. A barely perceptible tension tugged at Will's cheek. "Growing up, my mom added a note of compassion and levity around the house, which complemented my dad's austere nature. But after her death, my dad retreated into himself and his work."

"What happened to your mom?"

"Fatal gunshot ruled as an accident."

An awkward silence fell between them.

Annie finally asked. "Hunters?"

Will heaved a sigh. "Don't know, but if I hadn't stayed late after school, she would have been picking me up instead of at home when the bullet hit her. Blame haunted me."

"How awful. I'm so sorry."

"Dad never said her death was my fault, but I sensed an anguish coming from him that I couldn't explain any other way. His counsel was to accept what happened and be a man, which to me meant I wasn't supposed to cry."

"It's not good to bottle up emotion."

"I cried but only at night into my pillow so my dad couldn't hear."

Will paused and ran his fingers over the moisture on the outside of his tea glass. The tragic loss of his mother put his concern over the shots fired in the woods in a different light. Annie resisted the urge to slide from her stool and hug him. Jelly Bean snuggled up against her leg, as if sensing the need for comfort in the room. Will surprised her and continued.

"One day the pent up misery took my feet to the end of our drive. I started running and didn't quit until I was spent and numb. My neighbor saw me and said running must be God's way of showing me how to live with the pain."

Compassion tugged at Annie's core. This special man chose to share his personal hurts with her. "What a beautiful picture of God meeting you in the midst of your pain. Do you still run?"

"No. That's the kicker. I turned out like my dad—a workaholic. When I graduated, he didn't press me to stay and take over the family farm, though. He was fine with me leaving. I chose law enforcement. School and work have been my life."

"Do you see law enforcement as a means of compensating for what you saw as failing your mother?"

He shrugged. "Maybe."

"I suppose we are similar in our goals to do something worthwhile to make up for past failings." Annie gestured with her fork and shot a piece of lettuce onto Will's plate. Annie covered her mouth.

Will picked up the morsel and popped it in his mouth. "Thanks."

Annie busted out laughing. Jelly Bean looked up, stared, and twitched his snout.

"I'm not sure how the conversation strayed to psychoanalysis," Will said. "But let's get back to our mission. Your assignment is to continue working as a waitress. And because of your public relations major, you've been asked to create substance abuse material. I do not like Shag putting a controversial spin on the wet/dry issue, but that's the sort of stuff reporters do."

"My research into the county's stand on alcohol use does involve the decision to be dry as opposed to wet."

"Stick to defining the difference between the two topics. I'm here to enforce the law as it is on the books and not debate."

"Something I don't understand is how a bootleg operation still exists with direct-to-consumer sales available on the internet?"

"Simple supply and demand economics. Smugglers purchase wholesale then undercut legal sellers. An illegal business can offer a good price, bypassing all the permits, licensing, and tax regulations. They offer convenience with no ID check, a system to bring in other illicit drugs, and a good secondary income."

"A win, win for the lawbreakers?"

Will snapped a breadstick in half and bit off a portion. "Until they're caught."

After they cleared dishes and Annie put on coffee, Will asked, "How is your research coming along?"

"Interesting. I pulled back copies of the *Sugarville Weekly Journal* on microfiche. Did you know Sweet County has had two other appointed sheriffs, both killed in the line of duty?"

"The men at the barber shop made certain I knew."

"More than twenty years ago, Sheriff Billings was found dead of a shotgun wound after answering a call on a remote county road. His predecessor, Sheriff Winchester, apparently lost control of his car and crashed in the same ravine I almost ended up in."

"That explains the Winchester Ravine name."

"Yes. And illegal whiskey sales were a hot topic at the time of their deaths. I came across an article about a Finley Brice who was to give testimony and ... Will, is he ...?"

Frowning, Will dried his hands on a hand towel. "That's my father. I'd like to see the article."

"Sure. You pour the coffee and take it to the living room. I laid out ideas for a brochure on the coffee table for you to look over. I'll locate the story and bring it to you."

In the dining room, opposite the pink jumpsuit project, Annie had organized paperwork into four stacks—drug characteristics, dangers of substance abuse, laws, and related county history. She located the photocopy of the article that mentioned Finley Brice and started down the hall to the living room with Jelly Bean clip-clopping behind her.

Will had unfolded one of the trifold examples she'd created. "I like this layout with the 'Did You Know' title."

"I'm partial to that layout too. Here is the article you wanted to see."

Jelly Bean snorted and made a strange, guttural sound.

Annie jumped. "What's wrong, boy?"

The pink pig sniffed to the left and right of the table, stepped back and tapped his hooves against the carpet, twisted and moved his nose side to side like a carpet sweeper. Then he bucked and twirled around.

"Good grief," Will said. "He must need to go outside."

"Come on, boy." Annie went to the front door. Jelly Bean pranced behind her, his hooves clicking on the wood floor.

On the porch, Jelly Bean stood and stared at her with his pink-lined black eyes.

"I thought you wanted to go out. Go ahead, it's ok."

Jelly Bean hesitated, then clattered down the steps into the front yard.

Annie turned around and bumped into Will's chest, throwing her off balance. Will grabbed her shoulders and steadied her. He was so close she felt his heartbeat and drew in his clean scent.

She said, "Sorry" simultaneously with him.

Their faces were inches apart. She stared at his lips, so close they made her own lips tingle. Was he going to kiss her? She closed her eyes, tilted her head upward and ... his phone sounded—the vibration running through her chest. Her eyes popped open.

Lines between his brows creased. "Are you okay?"

"Uh ... yes."

"You looked faint."

She shrunk back. A self-deprecating laugh gurgled from her throat in the awkward moment. "I ... I didn't realize you were right behind me. I was startled. Shouldn't you answer your phone?"

He pulled his phone from his top pocket where he'd stuffed the news article and looked at the screen. "The office. I need to take it."

Annie shrugged her understanding.

"What kind of problem?" he asked the caller.

Will pressed his lips together that had come oh so close to hers as he listened to the person on the other end of the phone.

"I'll be right there."

He dropped the phone back into his pocket. "I hate to eat and run, but there's a complainant at the jail. Something to do with turkeys."

"No need to explain."

"Mind if I borrow this news clipping?" He patted his pocket.

"No. Go ahead."

"Thank you for dinner. We'll talk soon." He hurried down the steps to his car.

"Be careful." The expression of caring concern her parents always advised slipped out in a whisper. And the cautionary words were as much for her as they were for Will.

"Jelly Bean, what a way to end the evening. I was mooning into his eyes like a lovestruck nut. How embarrassing."

Will's taillights disappeared into the night while Jelly Bean sniffed and pawed at something on the front porch.

"What did you find?"

Annie stooped down and picked up a piece of cardboard and flipped it over. Scrawled in red letters was the word STOP.

Will cranked the engine and backed past the scrutiny of the lion statues at the end of the drive. Their furrowed brows told him what he already knew.

Annie McAfee rattled him. He'd wanted to kiss her. Not smart. He was not thinking clearly.

He'd dated some in the past, but work and school had left no time to develop a relationship. He wasn't sure he knew how. Can you give what you don't have?

After his mother died, his father left him adrift in an emotionally repressed home. Will learned the value of hard work from his father but nothing to fill the emptiness or allay his guilt—the guilt that her life might have been spared if he hadn't stayed late at school. He'd kept those feelings between him and God. Being a lawman had allowed him to handle others' tragedies, cloaking his own inner turmoil.

He was a problem solver and had learned to operate unencumbered by emotions sneaking in. But tonight, unexpected internal thoughts rose to the surface. Annie disarmed him. Thank goodness, there was a problem at the jail.

A good lawman did not share but extracted facts from others. Telling Annie he'd cried and run to deal with the pain of losing his mother left him exposed. He'd never shared the raw emotions surrounding his mother's death.

And he knew nothing of his father backing out of testifying at a hearing. What was he to testify to?

Will took a minute to stop beneath a streetlight and pulled the *Sugarville Weekly Journal* article with his father's name from his pocket. The brief story was titled: "Testimony Turnabout."

Illegal whiskey sales have been a hot topic in Sugarville since the debate about voting to keep it a dry county. Finley Brice, who was slated to testify in a hearing for the state looking into corruption in Sweet County, now claims he has nothing to testify to. Brice's wife died recently in what was ruled a hunting accident. But questions still remain, considering this is not hunting season.

He'd quashed the questions surrounding his mother's death. But seeing his father's name in print, along with the mention of hunting season, hit like a gut punch. Not wanting to testify right after losing his wife was understandable. But why was he scheduled to give testimony to begin with? How could his father have any role in the illegal activities in Sweet County? Where did a stray bullet come from if it wasn't hunting season? The quagmire begged for answers.

Will stuffed the article back in his pocket, disquieted by the irony that twenty years later, Will had a role to play in Sweet County—both he and Annie. Two divergent independents with a common goal—uncovering and eradicating illegal activity in Sweet County.

He'd crossed a dangerous line, even if only thinking about and not acting on his desire to kiss Annie. Depending on where they were and who they were with, he had to gauge how he behaved toward her. And no scenario allowed for kissing.

Will could not afford being sucked into an ocean of emotion. He had to take one problem at a time. And the current problem had to do with turkeys.

Minutes later, Will walked into the sheriff's office, and Pee Wee nodded toward the man seated in the reception area. He had a head of white close-cropped, coarse curls that contrasted with his ebony skin.

"I'm Sheriff Brice. You're waiting to see me?"

The man rubbed his hands on his jeans and stood. "Yes, sir. I'm Dilbert Clark."

Will offered his hand and received a handshake from the man's calloused hand that spoke of years of hard work.

"Sorry to bother you like this, but my wife insisted—"

"No need to apologize. You can see me any time. Come into my office."

Inside, Will motioned for the man to have a seat and went behind his desk. "I understand you have a complaint against my deputy?"

"Well, sir. I hate to complain, but I raise turkeys. I heard some commotion in a wooded section near my back fence, and that big deputy of yours shot the heck out of three of my turkeys."

"Did you talk to him?"

"No, sir. He was busy loading the turkeys into his car."

Will clicked the button on the intercom. "Pee Wee call Tommy and tell him to come to the sheriff's office right away."

In less than ten minutes, Tommy arrived.

"You wanted to see me?"

"Have you been shooting turkeys?"

"Not on duty. I just finished my shift and saw some wild turkeys come out of the woods. I took 'em to my apartment. My landlady was helping me clean them when you called."

Will closed his eyes briefly and shook his head. "Tommy, meet Dilbert Clark. He raises those turkeys you shot."

Tommy's eyes widened. "You raise turkeys?"

Dilbert nodded.

"I thought they were wild." Tommy stood frozen, as if facing a firing squad.

"Of course, Tommy will make restitution."

Tommy blinked. "I'll return 'em. Right away."

"No. I just want to be sure you don't shoot no more."

"No, sir. No more. I am sorry."

"Tommy will pay for the turkeys, whatever price you put on them. Will that be satisfactory?"

"No need—"

"Please." Tommy dug in his back pocket for his wallet. "I'll pay you, or no way I'd enjoy turkey dinner." Tommy pulled some bills from his wallet and placed them in Dilbert's hand. "That cover it?"

"Yes, sir, more than enough."

Tommy wrapped his big arm around Dilbert's shoulders, dwarfing him. The man's dark face turned a little gray. "How would you like to join me for dinner?"

Will intervened. "Mr. Clark probably eats plenty of turkey, since he raises them. Let him be on his way."

Tommy released him. "Oh sure, sorry."

"Thank you, sheriff."

Dilbert left.

"Tommy, one more thing. It's not hunting season."

"Wild turkeys aren't like wild hogs?"

"No. And you know the saying about ignorance being no excuse. Consider this a warning, and don't let it happen again. Close the door on your way out."

"Yes, sir."

The door closed. Will pulled the folded copy of the news article from his pocket, unfolded and carefully smoothed it flat on his desk. If only he could resolve the questions he had about his father as easily as a turkey dispute.

CHAPTER 17

Stop? Stop what? The other notes Annie had received related to her search for the truck that ran her off the road. She held onto the corner of the 'stop' note scrawled with what appeared to be red lipstick on a piece of cardboard.

Her gaze darted in all directions around the porch. Like the crack of a whip, lightning streaked the graying sky followed in seconds by thunderous rumbling. Jelly Bean's piggy tail tightened, and he pushed close to her leg.

Annie leaned down to give him a reassuring pat, her hand jerking when her phone sounded. "Jelly Bean, I'm jumpy too."

Nettie Sue launched straight into conversation, leaving off extraneous greetings or stating her name. "We're on our way. Tests took a long time. I figure we'll be back in about an hour. Had to stop for gas."

"Ok. Drive carefully, we have a thunderstorm developing here."

"During a thunderstorm, Jelly Bean does best if shut in his kennel. I packed the blanket he snuggles in during bad weather in the bottom of his food bag."

"I'll make sure he's comfy."

Without a goodbye, Nettie Sue ended the call.

Annie checked her screen, double-checking to make sure the call was no longer connected. "Your master does not waste words. Come on, boy."

Light sprinkles of rain spattered the porch railing and more thunder rumbled in the distance. Inside, Jelly Bean ducked into his kennel. Annie found his soft, pale blue, cuddly blanket with a sweet scent.

"Here you go." She placed the blanket in the kennel and fastened his cage door. Jelly Bean nuzzled the blanket, rearranging its folds with his snout until he was surrounded by a puffy cloud of security.

Annie searched in the pantry for a large paper bag and dropped the new piece of evidence inside. "What am I supposed to stop? I doubt waitressing or pig sitting is the issue."

Jelly Bean shifted in his kennel, and one eye peeked at her through the fluff of blanket.

Was her continued search for the person who ran her off the road the problem? She'd taken down a tag number. Had someone seen her? Maybe. She'd been researching underage drinking and the dangers. "People needed that information. Right?"

Jelly Bean's ear twitched.

The rain fell in earnest now. Fat raindrops pummeled the windows—a steady rain that could lull a person to sleep when safe indoors.

"Jelly Bean, I have my own favorite blanket to snuggle in while we wait on Nettie Sue." She plugged her phone into the charger on the kitchen counter and went upstairs.

Wrapped in her FSU garnet and gold blanket, Annie lay motionless, sprawled across her bed, preferring to remain in darkness. Windy gusts slung sheets and rain against the windowpane, then died down to a rhythmic pelting rain. Cozying into the softness of her blanket, she let her mind imagine pressing in close to Will. His scent reminded her of cutting into a fresh lime. Earthy, tangy. Would his lips be flavorful?

A thunk.

Jelly Bean? The sound became a creak, like a door opening slowly in an old black and white mystery movie. Jelly Bean's cage door? No, she'd secured the door to his kennel.

She sat up and snapped on the bedside lamp. Flashes of lightning momentarily lit the room. The lamp flickered and went out. The furnishings in the room became shadowy images. Something scratched at the window. She sat frozen to the edge of the bed. Another flash of lightning lit up the tree beside the house, revealing its branches scraping against the window.

She relaxed a moment.

Then clomp-tap thuds sounded on the wood floor. Footsteps. Someone was in the house. But how? She'd locked the doors. Hadn't she? She clutched the blanket close to her chest. Her heartbeat drummed in her ears.

If someone was in the house, she had to act. Her phone was downstairs. She'd left her gun in the glove compartment of the car. Stupid. Some undercover agent.

Her father had a handgun. The key to the gun cabinet was on a hook behind the dresser in the master bedroom. Annie rolled off the bed. She crept barefoot down the hall to the master bedroom, eased the door open, and closed it behind her. In the dark, she unhooked the key from its hiding place. Her hand bumped against cords plugged into the electric outlet, flipping the key from her fingers. She groped in the dark, straining at an awkward angle, feeling for it. The key lay somewhere buried in a grave of electronic cords.

Don't think graveyard.

She heard the clunk of footsteps in the downstairs hall, coming closer. A prickly sensation swept down her spine. Forget the gun cabinet key. She felt around her. What else could she use as a weapon?

She crawled on hands and knees to the side of the bed. Her mom's exercise weights rested on the bottom shelf of the bedside table. A light swept beneath the door. Annie picked up the eight-pounder.

The doorknob to the bedroom turned. A lightning flash highlighted the bathroom door. Annie scrambled to the bathroom and plastered herself behind the door with the weight clenched tight in her hand.

The bedroom door opened. A light momentarily swept across the bathroom. Annie's pulse raced, her breath shallow.

Drawers scraped open. The closet door squeaked against its hinges. Hangers scraped across the rod in the closet. What could he or she be looking for?

Brring

The doorbell. Nettie?

Muttering. A man's voice. The intruder moved out of the bedroom and heavy footsteps thudded against the stairs.

Annie eased from her hiding place. With the weight in hand, she inched into the upstairs hall.

A shadowy figure hesitated at the foot of the stairs. The doorbell rang again. A lightning flash silhouetted a heavyset man wearing a ball cap. He moved stealthily down the hall toward the back door.

Annie crept down the stairs. The intruder neared the back door. Jelly Bean squealed. The intruder's arms flailed. With a surge of energy, Annie lifted and hurled the weight, hitting his ankle.

He stumbled, cursed, and fell to his knees, smacking against the door frame. Jelly Bean's kennel rattled, and he screeched. A china platter hanging on the wall crashed to the floor. Grabbing the doorknob, the culprit snatched the door open and fled.

Jelly Bean pawed at the side of the kennel. Annie ran through the broken shards and leaped onto the porch. A hand grasped her shoulder out of the dark.

Will jammed the sheriff's vehicle into park and bounded out of the car.

It had taken only minutes to return to the parsonage after Nettie Sue's call, reporting that she couldn't get anyone to the door and had heard a loud crash inside.

When he saw Annie, chin in hands, seated on the top of the back porch stairs, relief ran through him. He wanted to scoop her in his arms and pick up where they'd left off on the front porch earlier, but propriety reigned. "Are you okay?"

"Yes, but bummed I didn't catch the guy. Nettie Sue came out of nowhere and scared me witless." Annie pressed a hand over her heart. "I'm just now reeling my heart back inside my chest."

"You tried to catch the intruder?"

"Come inside. The power just came back on." Annie stood and pushed the rear door open and pointed to a good-sized dumbbell laying on the floor in the middle of broken pieces of ceramic. "I tried to stop him with a weight, but it just threw him off balance. He broke grandmother's hand-painted platter. My mom is going to be upset."

A dumbbell to stop an intruder? Her creative gumption was a debatable virtue. "I think your mom would be more upset if you had been broken. What were you going to do with the guy if you caught him?"

"Find out if he left the 'stop' note Jelly Bean found."

"What are you talking about?"

"Follow me. Nettie Sue is in the kitchen calming Jelly Bean down. We've been careful not to touch anything so you can dust for fingerprints."

In the kitchen, Nettie Sue spoke soothingly to Jelly Bean, who was barely visible in a cloud of blue blanket inside his kennel.

Will nodded to her. "I appreciate you calling."

She shrugged. "It was the right thing to do. Jelly Bean don't like the dark or loud noises."

Annie opened a paper bag and used tongs to remove a piece of cardboard with STOP written in large red letters. "Someone left this by the front door, and Jelly Bean found it right after you left."

"What are you supposed to stop?"

"That's what I want to know."

Jelly Bean pushed out of his blanket and stood, wiggling his snout.

"He's ready to go out," Nettie Sue said, and opened the kennel.

Jelly Bean stepped out and trotted through the broken glass to the rear door. He stopped, sniffed, made guttural grunts and pawed at the floor.

"He did that earlier tonight," Will said.

Nettie Sue turned and eyed Will. "You smoke?"

Her question set Will back. "Smoke? No."

"Jelly Bean alerts on all kinds of smokes." Nettie Sue walked to the threshold, leaned down and pointed. "See?"

Will squatted beside her. In the crevice of the threshold was a hand-rolled cigarette.

Annie peered down at the find. "The guy who broke in must have dropped it."

"Cigars. cigarettes, joints. Jelly Bean will find 'em. I don't allow smokin' around Papa. He's on oxygen, and it's flammable."

"How did Jelly Bean learn to sniff out cigarettes?"

"I watched how on YouTube. He expects a treat when he finds something. Do you have any apple slices?"

"No wonder Jelly Bean stared at me when I put him outside earlier. Mr. Fleming must have smoked in the living room where Jelly Bean had a prancing fit." Annie went to the refrigerator, retrieved and sliced an apple for Nettie Sue to reward Jelly Bean.

Will used Annie's tongs to retrieve the cigarette, and she handed him a small paper bag, and a pen to label the latest evidence.

Jelly Bean went out in the yard, and Nettie Sue continued to explain how she trained Jelly Bean.

"I took Jelly Bean to places where teenagers had partied or hung out to find discarded cigarette stubs and such. I'd let Jelly Bean smell them, then hide the items. When he sniffed them out, he got a treat."

Jelly Bean climbed back onto the porch. Nettie Sue stroked the pig's head. "He got to where he'd dance around in a circle when he found something. He's an excellent sniffer."

Astonishment crept over Will. If Jelly Bean trained on debris left behind after teen gatherings, it was likely that Jelly Bean could sniff out more than tobacco.

CHAPTER 18

Could this be the day he'd learn from his father the truth behind his mother's death? Will patted his pocket, making certain he had the news clipping Annie had given him.

With sheriff's department duties handled and Annie's house on extra patrol, Will crossed the county line into Hill County.

After his mother died, his father had remained at home physically, but mentally and emotionally he'd abandoned Will. An invisible wall had formed, separating him from his father.

Rolling down his windows, Will breathed in the fresh, pine-scented air, reminding him of happier days camping with his mother and dad.

One trip, they'd set up camp beside a small creek off the Chipola River. What they had for dinner depended on the fish caught, and they ended up dividing one fish three ways. His mom cooked a pot of grits to help fill their tin plates. Laughter came easily then.

When Will had called his father this morning, his dad seemed pleased and said he had a pot of greens already cooking. He might not be so pleased, however, when Will questioned him about the news clipping. A whispered prayer crossed his lips.

"Lord, I need direction—the words to say to elicit answers from my father."

The approach leading to Wildflower Road and the family farmhouse had changed little. The corner gas station had tacked on a convenience store, which would have been handy instead of having to drive the eight miles into town to go to the grocery store.

His stomach tightened as he made the same turn the school bus made the day his mother was killed.

He had stayed after school for a Future Farmers meeting that turned out to be a waste of time. The president was absent, and the teacher sponsor said he'd get word out about the proposed new slate of officers for the following year in homeroom. He had taken the late bus provided for students who had extracurricular activities.

When Will stepped from the bus, a hint of red glinted through the trees, which turned out to be an ambulance sitting alongside a sheriff's car in the farmyard.

Two men in white uniforms put a sheet-covered stretcher in the rear of the ambulance. He could not see who was underneath the sheet.

The scene made his limbs go weak. "Mom? Dad?"

Hands touched his shoulders. Mrs. Smith from the neighboring farm. "Honey, your father asked me to come over to be with you when you got home."

His father stood behind his truck, the tailgate down. The deputy was talking and gesturing toward the gun rack in the truck.

The contents of a grocery bag lay scattered on the ground. A bunch of celery, milk, a head of lettuce, a sack of flour, a bag of marshmallows, and a can of peaches lay in disarray in the dirt behind the ambulance.

"I'm making peach cobbler tonight." His mother had made the statement in a happy sing-song voice as she cleared the breakfast dishes before he left for school.

His father had eaten breakfast early and left on the tractor to plow new ground in the north field. "I'm going to the store for supplies for our next camping trip. Anything special you want me to pick up?"

"Can you get marshmallows?"

"Good idea." She gave a silly smile he had no way of knowing was the last happy facial expression he'd see her make. "We can roast them for dinner if we only catch one fish."

"What's happened? Where's my mom?"

"Let's go in the kitchen. Your father is busy. He'll talk to you shortly."

Eventually, his dad did walk into the kitchen, and Mrs. Smith left.

"Where's Mom?"

His father stood in front of the kitchen sink and stared out the window into the backyard. "Your mother was accidentally shot and killed."

An invisible weight enveloped him, sucking the air from Will's lungs.

His father kept his back turned to him, his hands clinging to the edge of the sink. "You'll have to be a man quicker than most."

Giggles, laughter, and smiles ended that day. Home shifted to a quiet household with his father—already a man of few words—speaking even fewer.

Will turned off Wildflower onto Brice Farm Road. The dirt road had earned a sign, but not pavement. His tires kicked up a dust cloud on the road where he used to run.

He pulled into the clearing next to the farmhouse and parked, avoiding the spot where his mother had died. Grass, though mowed, had taken over the ground where the groceries had spilled twenty years before.

Will heaved a shaky sigh and climbed the concrete steps leading to the kitchen. He was greeted with the strong odor of collard greens and ham hock cooking on the stove. An iron skillet of lightly browned cornbread sat cooling on the counter.

Will's father grabbed a dish towel and wiped at his hands before grasping Will's hand. "So glad you took time to come see me."

"Yes, sir. This job has me in closer proximity."

They ate and chatted about mundane matters—his father's latest planting of field peas and corn, the hot weather, and the need for rain.

"How are things going for you in Sweet County?"

"Busy." Not wanting to delay his primary purpose in coming any longer, Will dusted cornbread crumbs from his fingers and pulled the clipping from his pocket.

"I am dealing with a teen drinking problem, and a volunteer is researching the issue to develop educational material. This clipping surfaced." He pushed the dishes aside and laid the news article on the table.

The pleasant look on his father's face tightened. He read silently, then looked up and stared at Will. "What do you want me to say?"

Will shrugged.

"You think I shot your mother?" His father pushed back from the table. The scraping sound of the chair legs grated across Will's raw nerves.

"I don't know what to think."

His father dropped his head and pressed his palms against his face. Will waited—a technique he'd learned when questioning someone. A suspect would eventually say something to fill in an uncomfortable silence. Was he going to make a confession? His father pushed himself up, using the table to assist him, and finally spoke.

"There was talk, rumors, and questions revolving around your mother's death—whether it was accidental. As you know, a husband is an automatic suspect. They test fired the rifle I kept in my truck to compare it to the fatal bullet and found it was not a match. The only thing I can tell you for sure is that I didn't do it."

"I need to know the *whole* truth. What were you testifying to? Why did you back off? Did you take a payoff? Let someone bully you? Were you blackmailed?"

His father abruptly turned away and leaned against the sink with his back to Will. The same way he had stood the night he told Will his mother was dead. He spoke in a low, steady voice. "Listen to me. For your safety, don't delve into the corruption in Sweet County."

A flush of anger swept through Will. "What? I'm the sheriff. It's my job, at least for the time being."

His father pushed against the sink and whirled around. "Exactly." His eyes were aflame with what? Fear? Concern? Anger? Emotions from his father he'd never witnessed before.

"For the time being, it's your job. But it doesn't have to be. Will, leave Sweet County. Go back to your state job."

CHAPTER 19

Facing the room of senior English students minus Adam Beck, Annie jiggled her knee and waited for Cora Neddles to complete the classroom business of taking roll and making announcements.

It had been two weeks since the intruder scare. Will had his men provide the parsonage with extra patrol, but she'd seen little of Will until a few nights ago when she'd typed two search warrants for him.

"The computers returned to the department are too dated to handle scans and forms," he'd said. "I had to resort to using a typewriter with no spell check. The circuit judge returned my search warrants with errors to be corrected in red." He'd grumbled about the judge not allowing him to initial corrections and said he felt like he was back in English class.

She'd missed *him* but he apparently had no problem staying away from *her* the last couple of weeks.

The clang of lockers and sweet-smelling floor compound at Sugarville High School transported Annie to her high school years. Her senior year was not so long ago she had forgotten how difficult it could be to reach teens.

Annie had done the research, spelled out the facts with bullet points, then prayed for God's direction on how to present the material in a meaningful way. The answer came in her sleep.

Show them.

She had called Ms. Neddles before school this morning with her idea.

"Ms. McAfee is a recent communication graduate from Florida State University," Ms. Neddles began her introduction, "and has been recruited to develop educational materials on substance abuse for our sheriff's office. She will be sharing important information with us today." Ms. Neddles turned to Annie. "They all have name placards on their desks for you as you requested. You have the floor."

The classroom held five rows of desks with six students in each row. Annie spotted Adam's empty seat—fifth row second from the end by the windows.

She began without words. Walking past each aisle, she silently read the student's name on each desk, took in each face staring curiously at her, then stopped at the end of the fifth row.

"Class, I'm not here to lecture you while you sit in your seats."

"Good," one boy said, eliciting giggles throughout the room.

"I'm here to talk to you about *this* empty seat."

A hush fell over the room. Some looked at the boys— Clint, Hudson, and Larry—all sitting in the fourth row. Clint sat stiff and still. Hudson put his head on his desk. Larry fidgeted in his seat and wiggled his right foot crossed over his left knee. Annie had everyone's attention.

"This empty seat joins with thousands across the country who have already lost their lives. Sadly, odds are there will be many more empty seats."

"Sue," she asked the girl on the back of row three, "when there is an epidemic, what do scientists and people who are interested do about it?"

The girl raised her shoulders and gave the answer as a question. "Research?"

"Exactly. Research provides a lot of statistics about the dangers of drug abuse, whether legal or illegal. I could tell you that eighty percent of teens who drink alcohol or take drugs do so without considering the risks, but I doubt you'll remember that statistic like you will Adam's empty seat."

Annie stepped over to the third row. "Billy, I could tell you alcohol is the most widely abused substance used by teens, but the impact of that statement is less likely to stick with you than that empty seat." Annie motioned to the seat with her head.

Billy bit his lower lip and nodded.

"Would anyone like to venture a guess as to why teens drink or do drugs?"

She received a variety of responses from "nothing else to do" to "wanting to fit in." Hudson said, "poor decisions."

"Yes." Annie walked over to the empty chair and rested her hands on the back of the desk. The entire class fell silent. "Alcohol and drugs can alter the brain's structure and function because the brain is not fully developed until age twenty-five. And there's one more thing no one has mentioned. It's illegal."

Mike raised his hand, and Annie called on him. "I think making alcohol illegal to sell in Sweet County, which is supposedly dry, entices teenagers to see what they can get away with." Annie noticed Hudson poke Larry in the back.

"Yeah, what's up with that?" A boy named Johnny, who had been quiet, spoke up. "Drinkers don't stop drinking in a dry county. They go to a wet county and bring it back or get it under the table from locals."

"Yes, and locals can charge whatever they want to whoever they want," Annie said.

"So, do you think we should change from a dry county?" Hudson asked.

"In wet counties, sales are regulated and ages checked, which I believe could curtail underage drinking. What do you all think?"

Susan raised her hand. "If we had been a wet county, maybe Adam's seat wouldn't be empty."

"Maybe. But is wet or dry really the issue? Young people all over this country are dying not because of where they live but because of what they choose to put in their bodies. My challenge to each of you is to take care of *your* bodies and make sure there are no more empty seats."

Will pulled into Rex's service station. The afternoon boasted of clear blue skies with the promise of a temperature destined to keep rising. Will used his handkerchief to wipe the moisture from his forehead and neck and spoke to Rex, who exited the gas station office.

"Have time to service my patrol car?"

"You picked a good day to bring 'er in." Rex pointed to the car lift in his garage. "Bud Dillman's working with me today. He comes in once or twice a week to help out."

"I thought he was an auto body man."

"Works on insides and outsides."

Tommy wheeled his patrol car into the station and parked beside Will, "Sheriff, I'm at your service while your car's being serviced." Tommy spotted Bud Dillman and tipped his hat.

Bud stopped what he was doing, stared a moment, and then went back to work underneath the car on the rack.

"I guess he isn't over my testing his rifle after you questioned his son about that coon hunt shooting incident."

Rex shrugged. "Bud's not so good with cordialities, you know?"

"I reckon I do." Tommy dusted his Stetson against his knee. "Sheriff, I tracked down a shooting range. A worker at Redfern Farms said there is a place on the south end of the county that's kind of hilly and has a natural embankment."

"That's right." Rex closed his lazy eye and made a pistol with his hand. "The big ridge on the left just before you reach the county line makes a good place to shoot. I zeroed in my rifle out there."

"Good to know." Will had promised to take Annie to shoot with her father's .357 magnum after the intruder break-in. Target practice would give him another good excuse to spend time with her. After the almost kiss, he'd felt it best to keep his distance and adhere to legitimate business purposes to see her. Asking her to type the search warrants Judge Hallerton refused to sign gave him a credible reason to see her a few days ago. And tonight, she'd invited him to dinner to hear how her presentation went at the high school.

Since the disappointing meeting with his father, Will had buried himself in work. The officers on loan from Tallahassee had completed their tasks and departed, and Will established a work schedule that covered patrol and radio communication needs on a rotation basis.

But Annie still had a way of sneaking into his thoughts. 'Remarkable' best described Annie McAfee. On the night she had typed the warrants, Annie had not only designed and produced a professional-looking brochure on substance abuse, but she had also presented him with four new pink jumpsuits for the jail. No wonder FDLE saw her as a valuable asset.

"When can my car be ready, Rex?"

"With Bud here, we should have you fixed up in an hour or so."

Will grabbed an envelope from his car seat. "Thanks for the ride offer, Tommy, but the courthouse is only one block over. I'll walk back and pick up my car when I'm finished with my business."

The short walk to the courthouse gave him time to mull over the latest developments. His father's entreaty for him to quit a couple of weeks ago swept over him with a brushstroke of defiance. How could he suggest Will tuck tail and run like his father apparently had? What happened? What could his father possibly have known back then? What made him clam up? He'd chickened out on whatever the prosecution needed, and now his father asked him to do the same. No way. His father's mindset rankled him. But after twenty years, did he really expect anything different? Ultimately, his father's attitude fueled his determination to carry out the mandate to clean up Sweet County.

When he checked on his undercover agents, Sylvester had patted Will on the back in congratulations. "You will be elated to know you have a healthy hooch market in your dry county and a thriving numbers racket to boot." According to Sylvester's contacts, Will was biding his time and looking the other way rather than dealing with illegal activity.

Elated? No. Burdened? Yes. Sweet County offered an island oasis for underage drinking, cheaper prices, and a proven system for sales. Their readymade supply chain produced an easy means of distribution for other drugs like the pot and fentanyl that had shown up in Adam's body.

Since Will had learned about the pay to play agreement to operate bolita from Rufus Tate, he'd wondered how deep the corruption went. He set up a test run to see if word got out about the search warrants prior to service. Last night validated his suspicions.

Tommy had witnessed teens handing money in exchange for brown-bagged items at the places they served the warrants. But their searches yielded a couple of baskets of dirty clothes on the utility porch of one house and a bag of charcoal and grill equipment at the other.

News of the warrants had leaked like a new puppy.

CHAPTER 20

Annie finished tying on her apron and pushed through the cafe's two-way kitchen door.

"I'm glad you're here," Candy said. "Linda Lynn is handling the orders, but it's getting busy." Candy released the beaters from the mixer used to whip potatoes and placed them in the sink to soak. "How did the presentation go this morning?"

"The students were attentive and participated."

"Good. Now you can focus on food." Candy handed Annie two, covered food containers. "Put two sweet teas with these blue plate takeouts Jessie ordered and tell Linda Lynn that Sara Jane and Juanita's orders are ready."

Annie delivered the message to Linda Lynn. "Thanks. Can you take the Redfern's order? They just came in."

On her way to the Redfern's booth in the corner, Annie spoke to Sara Jane and Juanita seated at their usual window table. "Linda Lynn is bringing your order out." She greeted Mayor Alton Fox in the booth behind them and smiled at Mr. and Mrs. Spradley from the florist shop seated at a table in the center of the room.

"Good afternoon, Mr. Redfern and Mr. Redfern."

Al Redfern raised a friendly hand. "Please, call me Al. Have you met my brother Art?"

"I have ... at the fair. Good to see you again. I purchased manure and mulch for the parsonage rose garden at your farm a few weeks ago."

"I hope you were treated right."

"Yes, sir. And the garden is doing well. What can I bring you?"

Annie took their order for burgers and fries and turned it in to Candy just as Lessie arrived to pick up the takeout meals.

"Well, I hear you've been a busy girl today."

Annie looked behind her. "Are you talking to me?"

"Yes," Lessie said. "Is it true you were promoting a wet county at the high school this morning?"

"I spoke to a senior English class, and a student brought up the subject." She set the to-go containers out for Lessie. "How did you hear?"

"One of the students went home for lunch and told her mother. Jessie is giving a perm to the mother right now."

"Ah. The beauty shop quick news release."

"More tea, please," Sara Jane called from her seat.

"You go ahead. I'll grab a drink carrier for the tea." Lessie said.

Annie picked up a full pitcher of tea and refreshed Sara Jane's and Juanita's iced tea.

"You were debating about having a wet or dry county at the high school?" Sara Jane asked.

"My topic was underage drinking and substance abuse. The benefits and drawbacks of wet and dry counties came up."

"I suppose the teens want a wet county," Juanita sniffed.

"What the teens want are no more empty seats in their classroom like the one Adam Beck left behind. Besides, from what I've been reading, changing to a wet county with its regulations could help curb underage drinking."

A gasp erupted from Juanita.

"You can't mean that," Sara Jane said. "If you only knew how hard we have fought to keep our county dry. We want a peaceful, nice place to live. Not liquor stores on every corner and the riffraff that would bring. Aren't you the pastor's daughter?"

"Whoa. Time out. I'm just saying there are two sides to this argument, and maybe people should be open to both."

"Don't worry, we heard the arguments the last time it came up for a vote." Mr. Spradley spoke from the table behind Annie and turned to Al Redfern. "How long has it been since you presented before the commission?"

Al looked at his brother as if to ask if he knew. He lifted his shoulders and shook his head. "Maybe ten years. However long Sheriff Daly was in office," Art said.

Mayor Fox spoke up. "I know kids will be kids. But keeping us dry will at least make it harder to buy alcohol, and we won't be bothered with the visible influence."

With the talk against a wet county swirling around her, Annie retreated behind the counter, secured the lids on the to-go cups of iced tea, and placed them in the drink carry tray for Lessie.

"You ready to take my money?" Lessie asked.

Annie rang up the ticket, put her money in the cash drawer, and counted out her change. "Looks like my good intentions led to unintended backlash."

"Sorry," Lessie said softly. "I shouldn't have blurted what I heard. But—my advice—" Lessie cut her eyes toward the group behind her, "if you have anything good to say about becoming a wet county, keep it to yourself."

The wooden floorboards squeaked under Will's footsteps on the way to the clerk's office in the century old Sweet County Courthouse. Will stood aside for a couple leaving the office with eyes only for each other and a paper in hand—a marriage license?

Inside, Susan Busby, who had stamped the affidavits for the search warrants served over the weekend, met him at the counter. She hooked a long straight strand of sandy blonde hair behind her ear and positioned her wire-rimmed glasses on her nose. "Good morning, sheriff. How did you do with your searches?"

Will placed the return service paperwork on the counter and offered a disheartened smile. "We didn't do so well."

She scrunched her brows together. "You didn't find anything?"

"No. My next stop is to let the judge know the results. Have you seen him around?"

"Not since lunch, but his secretary will know where he is."

Will continued to Judge Hallerton's office. A nameplate for Pam F. Reston sat on the desk in the outer office, but she was not present. He reached to remove a business card from its holder on the desk when a voice with a suspicious edge sounded behind him. "Can I help you?"

"You must be Pam. You weren't here when I was in to see the judge last week. I'm Sheriff Brice. Is the judge in?"

Her face turned from suspicious to saccharine. "Sheriff. Nice to meet you. I must have been running an errand for the judge. There's more to do around here than sit behind the desk." Her words dropped defensively, as though she had taken his remark as a backhanded criticism.

She set a coffeepot filled with water on her desk and flipped to a page in her planner. "He has a hearing in his chambers right now." She glanced at the clock on the wall. "I doubt he'll be much longer. Coffee? I'll have it made in short order."

"Thank you. I'll take you up on the offer."

Pam disappeared into a small alcove behind her desk, and he could hear sounds of coffee preparation. The pad on her desk had doodle marks of arrows and dollar signs. A sticky note attached to her phone read: Call S. B. with an exclamation point.

Will took a seat.

She returned and sat at her desk. "How do you like the sheriff job?"

"Truth be known, I'm a little disappointed right now."

She lifted her brows in question. "Really?"

The door to the judge's office opened. A man accompanied by a teenage boy stepped out, followed by the judge. Will stood.

"Well, we were just talking about you." Judge Hallerton said. "Sheriff, meet Mr. Fulton and his son Jared." Tension pulsed the air along with gurgling sounds from the coffeemaker.

Nodding, Will acknowledged the father and his boy, who Patrolman Newsome identified as being responsible for the Thornton hit-and-run accident.

Pointedly ignoring Will, the father lifted his chin and turned to Judge Hallerton. "I will hire an attorney for the trial."

"That's advisable," Hallerton said.

Mr. Fulton steered his son out of the office, avoiding eye contact with Will.

The judge handed a paper to Pam. "Put Jared Fulton on the docket for the next available juvenile court date."

Rubbing his hands together, Judge Hallerton asked, "How did you do with the search warrants?"

"We drew a blank. It appeared the Taylors and Alcourts knew we were coming."

The judge's forehead accordioned. "Oh?"

"Maybe they have a nose for smelling a rat—a sixth sense. Whatever the reason, we found nothing. I left the return service paperwork with the clerk's office and came here to let you know the results."

"I see." He slapped his hand on Pam's desk in what-a-shame fashion. "If I can be of help with any future warrants let me know."

"Thank you, sir."

The coffeemaker wheezed. "You want to wait on that coffee?" Pam asked.

"No, thanks. Maybe next time."

"Sure, next time," she quipped.

Leaving the office, Will fumed inside. Couldn't Jared's father see that covering for his son was doing him a disservice? And what about the judge meeting with the boy and his father prior to a trial? Pieces of a puzzle spelling trouble were fitting together. Gone were the days of kids sneaking beer and whiskey being a harmless tradition worthy of a wink and a reprimand. Fentanyl showing up in Adam's system proved Sweet County was not immune to illicit drugs.

Intent on retracing his steps down the hall, Will nearly collided with Marvin Borg, aka Shag, coming out of the men's restroom.

"Hi, Sheriff. I hear Ms. McAfee's presentation on substance abuse generated quite a controversy."

"Controversy? Did something happen I should know about?"

Shag's lips twitched like a dog anticipating a tasty tidbit. "Discussion about wet and dry counties. I'm sure Ms. McAfee will report her side to you. Care to comment?"

Her side? Now what? Trained to squeeze out information, Shag had laid the groundwork to stir up the wet-dry issue the way he'd headlined the article about Annie developing substance abuse materials. Like a game of tug of war, pitting one side against the other, he plied his trade to generate interest and sell newspapers. Will would not be sucked in.

"Shag, a local teenager is dead. My focus, and Ms. McAfee's, is warning teens on the dangers of alcohol and drugs. I'll wait to hear her side."

"Sure. I understand. Can you speak to your latest news?"

"You think I have news?"

"I just heard search warrants you served turned up nothing."

"The latest news is the town grapevine is alive and healthy." Will resumed his walk down the hall.

Shag scrambled after him, pencil and paper in hand. "That's good. Can I quote you on that?"

"Feel free," Will said, pressing the courthouse door push bar with a metallic thunk.

CHAPTER 21

Annie pulled her car to a stop on the steep drive of the parsonage and barely had the energy to set the brake. She was a stalk of corn in one of Sweet County's cornfields, singled out by a whirlwind and buffeted on all sides.

She usually viewed the Victorian house perched on the hill as stately with its steep gabled roofs, interesting nooks and crannies, and a wraparound porch, but today the ash-gray house blended into the overcast sky, matching her gloomy spirit.

Styled with a turret for a damsel in distress, architectural wood blocks decorated the top corners of all the windows, serving no other function than ornamentation.

Nonfunctional described how she felt. Sweet Countians wanted her to handle surface needs and provide no other function. They didn't want in-depth thinking of the dangerous issues and how to deal with them. The townspeople were only interested in window dressing and 'sweet' appearances.

She expelled a puff of breath, climbed the steps, and entered the house, trudging down the hall to the kitchen. With a quick flick of the wrist, the car keys clattered onto the tile counter. 'Misunderstood' should be a sign hanging around her neck. Who would believe a presentation to impart helpful, life-saving information for teens could upset the community?

Her dad preached about taking a day at a time and concentrating on the task at hand. "Don't draw attention to yourself unnecessarily. Do what is right and you can't go wrong."

News flash, Dad, doing good *could* go wrong.

"You're spending the summer in Sweet County?" her FDLE supervisor had said. "Perfect. You can be a help to local law enforcement and get the pulse of the community."

She had the pulse all right, pounding in her ears all afternoon. The confidence level of her supervisor might take a serious plunge.

Thankful she didn't have to cook, Annie placed the to-go dinners of meat loaf, mashed potatoes, and lima beans on the counter. The possibility of a quiet, stress-free dinner with Will had faded. She looked forward to seeing him but also dreaded telling him about the bitterness stirred up after her presentation.

How did she manage to draw out animosity and irritate people? Her day had gone from elevated to deflated, from winner to whiner, and she did not like herself.

Annie pulled a yeast roll and butter packet from the bag Candy had filled. She lathered butter on the roll and dropped a piece in her mouth. Closing her eyes, she let the morsel languish on her tongue a moment before biting into the yeasty goodness.

Snap.

Her eyes popped open. The rat trap?

Annie pulled a flashlight from the kitchen drawer and eased open the basement door next to the pantry. She pulled the string hanging from the light and the bare bulb lit the stairs but did little to reach the dark corners of the room. She'd placed the rat trap beside the wall across from the stairs.

There was a bumping sound. The critter? She steeled her shoulders and approached the wire cage she'd baited with cheeses and shined the flashlight inside. The bait remained in place and the trap door stood wide open.

Thump.

She whirled about, shining the light across the room. Nothing. Everything seemed in order. The snapping and thumping was coming from outside. The rose garden? At the café, Juanita had complained that deer were eating her snap pea buds. Would deer invade roses?

The basement window was too high to look out. Annie climbed the stairs that led outside. The door opened onto a concrete pad surrounded by a retaining wall with steps leading up to the rose garden at ground level. Strewn at her feet were crushed roses and branches. A rose stem flew over the wall, snagging her arm.

"Hey! Get outta here!" Annie scrambled up the steps and gasped at the sight. The garden was mutilated.

She felt a presence behind her just before a wallop hit the back of her neck. Jagged flashes blinded her vision and pain blazed through her body. She slumped to her knees as numbing static overpowered her hearing, and her world went dark.

The courthouse dome clock bonged five times. Will hurried down the courthouse steps to walk the one block to Rex's station. His phone vibrated, and Buzz Sinclair's name showed up on his call screen. Will answered and kept walking.

"I promised to contact you, buddy, as soon as I heard anything about the accreditation issue."

"What did you hear?"

"The ruling is official. Agents must have a college degree from an accredited program. At this point, guys like you and me with experience can request a waiver, but you must be currently on the force."

"How soon would I have to return in order to apply for the waiver?"

"ASAP. The cutoff date for waivers to be received is June seventh. I sent my waiver request in today."

"That's only one week."

"Exactly. If you want your old job back, I'd suggest you say goodbye to Sweet County, and let the governor appoint someone else."

Buzz's words still reverberated in Will's head when he pulled into the parsonage driveway. If he resigned, he'd make a lot of people in Sweet County happy, plus his father, and life would be simpler too.

Will was bombarded from all sides in Sweet County. Rex had to order new brake hoses for his sheriff's car to be installed next week. Although he had a detail working in secret, illegal suppliers perceived him as a pushover. His concern about leaks from the courthouse carried validity, and someone targeted Annie to stop something, for some unknown reason.

Then there was his attraction to Annie. Her strength, infectious smile, fresh-scented hair that grazed her shoulders, and the cute tilt of her chin when she talked caused emotions that he didn't know how to deal with.

He climbed the steps to the parsonage front porch, rang the bell and waited. The fragrant scent coming from the rose garden to the left of the porch permeated the air.

Annie's car was in the drive. Maybe she didn't hear the bell. He pulled open the screen door, rapped on the front door and waited.

He heard a faint sound. A voice? Was she calling for him to come in? He tried the door, but it was locked. He held the screen door steady to quiet its squeaks and listened.

He heard a voice again, or was it a moan?

"Annie?"

A definite groan came from the left side of the house. He scrambled down the steps. The rose garden was in shambles. Trampled branches covered the ground. Annie, hair askew and face ashen, struggled to stand at the top of the concrete basement steps. She wobbled. His stomach dropped.

"Annie, stay still." He spoke cautiously, not wanting to alarm her or make her move too quickly.

From her dazed look, he doubted she knew where she was or that she teetered on top of an eight-foot drop. One misstep could send her toppling over.

"Please, don't move." He made his way through the thorny tangle of bushes and crushed flowers.

Lord, steady her until I can put my hands on her.

He saw her knees give way. She swayed. Will jumped, grabbed her arms, and pulled her forward. She collapsed to her knees. Will squatted down beside her and wrapped his arms around her shoulders. Annie's body quivered. He held her close and lifted an urgent prayer. "Lord, be with Annie. Show me how to help her and to know what to do in this place that holds such hatred and destruction."

After a minute, her trembling subsided, and she reached for a broken rose stem. "The garden ..."

She lifted her head from his chest. "What happened?"

"I was hoping you could tell me." Will helped ease her into a sitting position. Earthy mulch odors mixed with the overly sweet fragrance of the crushed flowers. "When I got here, you were struggling to stand beside the basement steps, and the garden looked like this. What's the last thing you remember?"

"I ... I heard a noise. The rat trap. But there was no rat."

She closed her eyes and winced, as if recalling hurt her head.

"We better go inside. You can wait to talk."

She moved her head from side to side slowly, indicating she wanted to speak now.

"The noise was out here. Then someone ..." She touched the back of her neck and flinched.

Will brushed her hair aside. A red mark ran below her neck to the top of her shoulders.

"Someone hit you from behind?"

"I guess." She wiped away dirt from a bloody scratch on her arm and sucked in air, grimacing. "The last I remember, lights exploded like a jillion camera flashes going off at one time inside my head."

Will examined her forearm, the one without stitches from the attack at the fair. "Looks like this arm took the brunt of your fall. Can you move it?"

She lifted her arm and turned her wrist. "Hurts, but I don't think it's broken. I have matching wounded arms."

Hair fell across her face. Will reached up to move the hair away from her eyes and lightly tilted her chin up. "Annie, look into my eyes."

"Are you going to hypnotize me?"

He smirked. "You think I could have that kind of power over you?" Cupping her chin, he picked up the flashlight on the ground, and keeping the light low, checked her pupil reaction. Thankfully, the pupils constricted with the light. "I'm concerned with the fall and the blow from behind that you might have a head injury."

"You thought that already, didn't you?"

"That's a good sign if you can crack jokes."

He turned off the flashlight, set it on the ground, and placed his hands on her shoulders. "You gave me an awful scare. I'm thankful you're okay."

A strange look swept over her face. Her gaze locked on his in the deepening evening shadows, then her head dipped forward, eyes closed. Was she passing out? Her lips met his and a shaft of heat coursed through him.

She kissed him.

The thumping of his heart mingled with hers. Concerns over his father, the judge, and the worries of Sweet County evaporated like a raindrop in the hot summer sun. Amidst the strong fragrance unleashed by the roses scattered around them, he captured the sweetness of her lips and kissed her back.

CHAPTER 22

Located in a fresh, crisp-scented pine forest, the shooting range consisted of a natural clay embankment on a hillside at the end of a two-rut trail.

Will pulled Annie's target, smiled, and shook his head in admiration. The acrid bite of gun propellant hung in the air. She handled a gun with the stance and ease of a pro and managed to look lovely at the same time.

He held up the paper target for her to examine. "I'd hate to be on the receiving end of your aim when you're not bruised and banged up."

Her first shot was in the margin, but the next five rounds were dead center.

"You gave me good pointers." She weighed the weapon in her hand. "It's heavier than my .38 but a smooth shot once I adjusted to the feel."

Annie had insisted he take her to the shooting range for target practice with her father's .357 Colt Python. "The next time I check the rat trap, or somebody gets in the house, I guarantee I'll be packin'."

Will savored the taste of her tenacity and gutsy resolve. "Two-legged and four-legged trespassers beware."

Not only did she create a tight pattern on a target, but she'd also packed a wallop with her kiss. He found her strength intoxicating, yet her vulnerability spawned an enticing contradiction that made him want to protect and shield her.

It had been six days since the attack in the rose garden. She had suffered headaches, a sore neck and shoulders, scrapes and bruises. Candy had insisted she stay home the first couple of days after the incident, and she'd only worked single shifts the last few days.

Since it was a Monday in Sugarville, and businesses were closed, their afternoon was free. That morning Will had the brake hoses Rex had ordered installed. And he sent Tommy to Tallahassee to pick up the latest forensic analysis in Annie's case, which included another cut out letter note found in the massacred garden that read, *Kool it or you'll be crushed too.*

Annie sat on the bench fashioned from a wood plank on top of two sawed-off tree stumps and set the Python handgun beside her. "My dad and I talked about practice shooting, but we never did." She fingered the paper target a moment, then blurted, "I never grabbed someone and kissed them before. Will, I am so ... so ... sorry for latching onto you like I did. My dad calls it my FURI behavior. That is F-U-R-I, which stands for flaky, unthinking, rash, and impetuous."

"No reason to—"

She held up her hand "Yes. Yes, there is a reason. I need to explain. My dad, mom, and teachers worked with me to control my impulses but knowing and doing ... you know ... two different things."

"We all have our moments, besides—"

"Let me finish. I've worked hard to control my spur of the moment behavior. I can only attribute my wacky actions to getting knocked on the head."

Will lifted his hand. "Permission to speak?"

Annie grimaced and nodded.

"You can blame kissing me on your rattled brain and not knowing what you were doing. But I kissed you back and knew exactly what I was doing." Clasping his hands, Will leaned forward, resting his forearms on his legs. "Annie, the more I learn about you, the more I like you. You are courageous and willing to take a stand against popular thinking, but just as ready to unite with community thinking if required. I can open up to you like I never have to anyone. I'd be lying if I said I didn't enjoy kissing you back, but I know professional wisdom is to maintain a working relationship."

"Confession," Annie said. "I was not so addle-brained as to not know I liked kissing you. So, we're together on that front. And I understand your point about the working relationship. Can we try to tuck away those personal thoughts for a time when we are not directly working together?"

The way she made his heart pound when she looked at him wasn't normal. Not for him. But tempering emotion had been a staple of his life, thanks to his father.

Will stood to create distance. "A sensible solution. Your dad would be proud." *Return to a simpler subject.* "Do you feel more comfortable with the Python now?"

"I do." She patted the pistol. "But I'm not comfortable with the note we found in the wrecked rose garden. Someone wants me to not only stop something but to also cool it—with a K. I'd like to know what *it* refers to."

"When Tommy returns from the Tallahassee crime lab, I hope we'll have clues as to who and what's behind the threats."

"Do you think the scare tactics have something to do with the talk I gave at the high school?"

"Hard to say, could be. As long as we have humans, we are going to have differing opinions that multiply and spread." Will rubbed his forehead. "Sweet County's issues extended to my father in Hill County."

"Did your father give you an explanation about the testimony he was supposed to give?"

Will huffed out a tight sigh. "He clammed up and wouldn't talk. I'm convinced, after seeing that news clipping, something or someone has a hold over him. He apparently backed out of testifying to whatever he knew and wants me to back out of this assignment and leave Sweet County."

"Sweet County can leave a bitter taste."

"An astute thought that carries a lot of truth." Will packed the paper targets and earplugs in his duffel bag. "We better get going." He opened the passenger door for Annie and tossed the bag on the back seat of the patrol car.

A green and white sheriff's car pulled into the clearing. "Here's Tommy now. Wait here."

Will strode to the patrol car. Tommy handed Will a large envelope. "Habanero said to look at his test results, pronto."

Will looked over the analysis and saw why Habanero suggested he read the results right away. "Thank you for delivering this report—don't forget to check on that poker game this evening."

"You've got it, boss."

Tommy left and Will rejoined Annie.

"The lab found a fingerprint match on the notes directing you to the cabin and the one left in the rose garden, a different print was found on the message with the cash left on your car.

"Do they know who the prints belong to?"

"No, none of the prints were on file with the national or state database, and no prints were found on the 'stop' note, but it was written using lipstick, as you suspected."

"So, what does this tell us?" Annie cocked her head. "If the same person drafted the cabin and garden threats, there is an additional connection to explore.

"What do you mean?"

"The note we found in the garden spelled cool with a K like the Kool cigarettes found beside the cabin where we were shot at."

"Good point." Will raised his index finger. "I'm thinking out loud now. The cash with the warning and the message to go to the cabin concerned your search for the person who ran you off the road and had fingerprints from two different people. So, if the Kool it note relates to the cabin note, then the connection is your pursuit of the man who ran you off the road."

"Why smash the garden if I haven't been doing anything overtly to search for the guy who messed up my car?"

"Scare tactic. If the cabin and Kool it notes are linked, there may be more of a concern than just covering up who ran you off the road. Rather, the issue likely relates to the *reason* you were run off the road in the first place."

"Which is ...?"

"You are an outsider and somehow seen as a threat."

"Any threat to the traditions of Sweet County is not welcome?"

"Exactly. There are any number of people who are unhappy with me taking the place of their beloved sheriff and anything that goes against the establishment."

"Could the person who left the warnings be concerned with my substance abuse research and talking about wet and dry counties?"

"Possibly."

"What puzzles me is that the wet versus dry classification seems to be more of a worry than underage drinking to these people. Even after a local teen lost his life."

Will tapped the crime lab report on the car seat. "To further confuse matters, there's another finding listed in here that relates to Adam Beck's death. The boot print found behind the parsonage the night of the break-in matches the boot print found beside the pond at the golf course where Adam drowned."

Annie stared at him. "What could that mean?"

"We're dealing with a small town where connections and cross connections are more likely to occur. Our task is to find the common thread that links the factors to you."

"I can't imagine anyone could know about my FDLE connection, especially since my primary purpose in town really is to house sit and waitress this summer. My parents don't even know about my undercover work with FDLE."

"Whatever the reason, what we *do* know is you are a target. My asking you to compile substance abuse materials may have increased the threat to you."

"I don't get it."

Will released a heavy sigh, cranked the engine, and turned the car around. "Maybe there is no *getting* it. I've been in law enforcement long enough to tell you that there are simply some crazies out there who defy all explanations. In view of what's happened, it's time for me to act on the undercover operation."

He drove on the dirt trail back to the hard-top highway and turned toward town.

"The pine bluff made a perfect place to practice shooting. Thank you for taking me."

"No problem. I know who to call on if I ever need a sharpshooter."

"The way Sweet County is shaping up, the need for a sharpshooter is not a stretch."

"Agreed."

Annie shifted in her seat and leaned back against the headrest. "Wouldn't it be nice to be just normal people out for an afternoon drive to enjoy the countryside? I love the rolling landscape on this side of the county."

"The closer you are to Hill County where I grew up, the steeper the elevations."

"One thing I enjoy about the parsonage is that it sits on a hill."

Will crested a hill, and he applied slight pressure to the brakes. They gave little resistance. The speed increased. He pumped the brakes, and the pedal went to the floor. His chest tightened as the car continued to gain speed.

Annie straightened. "Will—"

"The brakes are gone."

A yellow caution sign with a black arrow indicated a sharp turn ahead.

"We'll never make that curve." Annie pressed her hands against the dash.

Will clamped down hard on the steering wheel with his forearms. With every muscle in his body taut, he kept his voice steady and firm. "Brace yourself."

Annie clutched the grab handle above the door and lifted a breathless prayer. "Lord God, somehow, some way, slow us down."

Careening toward the curve, options to slow down were limited. Will thrust the wheel to the right onto the grassy shoulder, peppered with large rocks. The tires plunged into the dirt, shooting plumes of rock and sand into the air. The car jettisoned, tilting as it went airborne headed toward a stand of trees.

Two wheels slammed to the ground. Will nearly lost his grip when the wheel jerked right and then left. Regaining control, Will worked the steering, frantically trying to keep the car from rolling over. The bottom of the car struck the ground with a pounding thud.

Two loud pops sounded. The air bags deployed. A mound of white punched him in the face, thrusting his head hard against the back of the seat. The car bucked, screeched, and continued to slide. With ears ringing and face stinging, Will's world spun in dizzying, star-studded circles that pulled him into a spiraling, magnetic, noiseless hole.

CHAPTER 23

Clomp-tap ... clomp-tap ... Footsteps. *The intruder was back?*

Annie lay perfectly still. The sounds advanced, retreated, then advanced again in a continuous rhythmic motion, like waves moving on and off a shoreline. Was someone toying with her? Playing a game?

A moan pricked her ears. Annie jerked her eyes open. The rumble in her throat told her the moan had come from her. All her body parts ached. Where was she?

A fan overhead clicked the lazy rotation of sounds she'd been hearing. A bit of light peeked under the drawn shades in the darkened room.

Pen, paper, and a Bible lay next to her on the bed. Slowly, she remembered she was in Lessie's guest room. Lessie had insisted she stay with her after the car crash. She had fallen asleep while searching Scriptures to help her deal with her hard-to-define emotions.

A knock came at the bedroom door.

"Annie, the sheriff will be here shortly," Lessie called to her.

Annie struggled to a sitting position. The air bags had left burning abrasions on her face, neck, and arms. "Okay."

Easing her stiff legs over the edge of the bed, she slipped into her sandals and opened the bedroom door. "I fell asleep."

"Good. You need the rest. I'll be in the kitchen making lemonade."

"Thank you. I'll be trying to make myself presentable."

Annie yawned, tried to smooth her hair, and winced when she touched the bruise on her head. She peered into the vanity mirror. Her bruises were a blend of blue to a reddish purple. She patted her cheeks, wishing she could borrow some of the color from her bruised forehead. Raising her arm slightly, she managed a bit of combing action, using her wrist without stressing her entire arm.

She applied a light pink gloss to her lips, and an impish grin inched the corners of her mouth. There was no forgetting the way she'd kissed Will, and he'd kissed her back, in the wrecked rose garden. Even after being hit in the head ... again. She brushed her fingers lightly over her lips reliving the dreamy feel of Will's lips on hers. The thought alone still stirred her spirit. But her jolted memory also hadn't turned loose of their agreement to tuck away romantic notions for now. Annie knew the decision was necessary due to their mission, but she couldn't deny strong feelings for Will smoldered within her heart. Putting those feelings away as they'd agreed wouldn't be easy for her. Would it be easy for Will?

After freshening, Annie joined Lessie in the kitchen. "Lessie, you're a doll to fix lemonade. Frosted glasses yet."

"Glad to do it. You both need a chance to relax. Sheriff Brice was uptight and more concerned about you than his own bruises and abrasions or his wrecked car."

"I'm fine, just sore all over."

"Well, don't overdo."

The doorbell rang.

Lessie peered down the hallway leading to the front door. "It's Will." She lifted the tray with the glasses. "I'll put this on the porch table so you and the sheriff can chat."

Annie greeted Will and held the door open for Lessie. "You can see I'm being spoiled. Lessie doesn't let me do anything."

"I knew you'd be in good hands." Will tried to take the tray.

"I've got this. You sit down. Both of you have orders to rest."

Annie sat in the chair. Will went to the porch swing. Lessie placed the tray on a wicker side table, then wagged a finger at Will. "I understand you went back to work anyhow."

"Guilty as charged." He touched the bandage on his forehead. "But I only had abrasions and a cut requiring a few stitches, not a concussion like Annie."

"You two take it easy." Lessie barked her command and went back inside, easing the screen door closed behind her.

Will handed Annie a glass of lemonade and took one for himself. "She's a combination drill sergeant and mom."

"A good description." The lemonade refreshed Annie's throat. Seeing Will and breathing in the perfumed air from the honeysuckle vine on the porch railing offered the first real comfort since the wreck. "Any news about the accident?"

"Yes. Gus says we were lucky to have come out of the accident alive and with only a battered exhaust system and fuel pump."

"Lucky maybe, but I expect prayer did the most good."

A smile drew across his lips. "I remember your prayer to slow us down."

His gaze warmed her cheeks. "That heartfelt prayer wasn't the only one sent heavenward. I talked to Mom and Dad yesterday, and they said they'd both felt the need to pray extra protection over me."

"Prayer, luck, whatever it was—the wrecker driver said the angle of the car wedged between the boulder and pine tree couldn't have been better planned."

"Angels."

"You believe in angels?"

"Certainly. My dad has preached on them. Angels are messengers sent to help us, and we are often unaware."

"Huh. Some of us must have more pull than others to get their assistance." Will set down his lemonade and pushed forward on his seat, making the swing chains rattle. "I have something I need to tell you."

She tensed at the sight of his resolute expression.

"I resigned as sheriff."

"What? ... No." Her heart rate sped up, making her already aching head throb.

He fanned his fingers out. "Hear me out. My friend, who is also a rookie at FDLE, warned me a few weeks ago the department was considering the requirement of a certified program in Criminal Justice or related field for employment. My buddy received his degree from the same on-line program I did."

"Your program wasn't certified?"

He shook his head. "The program was rigorous but inquiring about certification never occurred to me. I can request a waiver, but I have to be working as an agent for the request to be considered."

"Can't they classify this job as an FDLE special assignment?"

"No. I answer to the governor, not FDLE. And the governor is asking the impossible—to go against years of illegal gambling and whiskey trade. The people in this county don't want change. Unless they are affected negatively, citizens prefer to turn a blind eye to graft and support whatever maintains the status quo. I'm fighting a losing battle. My father was right. I should go back to the state job while I can."

"But the boy that died. The teen drinking—"

"I served search warrants where teens were seen buying alcohol. The searches came up with nothing."

"And you're quitting based on turning up nothing on two measly warrants?" Annie stood but her knees wobbled, and she clutched the arm of the chair.

"Whoa." Will grabbed her arm. "Lessie was right. You need to take things slow." Steadying her, he helped ease her back into the chair. "And Annie, there's more to my decision than the search warrants. Rex asked Reggie Dillman to put on the new brake hoses. Reggie claims he didn't have the proper tools to tighten the hoses securely and left to retrieve the wrenches from his father's repair shop. Rex assumed the job was finished and let me pick up the car."

"That's possible, isn't it?"

"Maybe, but Gus discovered more than loose brake hoses, there were cuts on the lines."

"All the more reason to fight back."

"No. All the more reason for me to quit. I never should have involved you in making the substance abuse materials, and I put you directly in harm's way riding in the patrol car. For your safety, my leaving is for the best."

LLY JO PITTS

She'd thought they'd shared a special bond. But kiss or no kiss, something did not feel right about what he was saying.

"Someone slashed your brake lines and you're quitting? I don't believe you. What happened to telling Shag, 'We're going after illegal sales.' What about the beverage agents you called in to help? You talked with such passion about people selling alcohol and drugs to teens and putting young people in danger. Was that empty talk? Are you—" Her voice strained and caught in her throat. She poked an accusing finger at him. "Are you going to let these people stay in control of Sweet County? Let them win?"

Will held up his hand. "You can stop right there."

"No." Annie rebutted with tears threatening. "Somebody wanted you dead, and if not dead, scared enough to quit." Tears streaked down her cheeks, and she swiped at them angrily with the back of her hands.

"You're going to hand them what they want? No fight? You'll be no better than your father, who apparently had information about illegal activity and chickened out. Think about what you're doing."

"I have. Both of us has said enough."

With that, Will bounded down the porch steps and didn't look back.

CHAPTER 24

Will parked in front of Bob's Barber Shop. Talking to Annie had been harder than he'd anticipated.

She'd struck a low blow, accusing him of being like his father. He had peeled off a layer of himself, and she'd used it to whack him over his very sensitive head. He gingerly touched the bandage covering his stitches.

Someone wanted him dead, and Annie had become collateral damage. Although she was alive and safe for now, the outcome could have been far different. Had Reggie or Bud Dillman deliberately vandalized his brakes because he'd questioned them about the shooting in the woods? Or had someone else accessed his car while left unattended at Rex's? Announcing he was leaving went against every principle he held dear. But he had to do what he was doing. This was the safest way for all involved, especially Annie.

Will forced himself out of the car and approached the barber shop door. Was he ready? He had to be.

Bob opened the door. "It's not locked, Sheriff, come on in."

Will stepped into the shop and breathed in the smells of soap and aftershave. Hank and Dave had their checkers game underway.

"Hop into the chair. You're my next customer."

"Hank and Dave were here before me."

"Those two don't count. They're part of the woodwork. Trim, shave? What are we doing today?"

"Trim is good, and I have some news you might be interested in."

"What news?"

"I'm resigning and waiting on the governor to send a replacement."

Bob tightened his grip on the cape he'd wrapped around Will's neck.

Hank, a checker in hand, halted his next move.

Dave's eyes popped. "You don't say."

Will stuck his finger between his neck and the cape. "Bob, give me a little breathing room, please. You'll be rid of me soon enough."

"Sorry." Bob relaxed his hold. "I thought you would stay awhile, so you caught me off guard."

Hank set down his checker. "Is it because of the failed search warrants?"

"And you know this how?"

Hank shrugged. "Sweet County grapevine."

"And the vine is so far-reaching law enforcement doesn't have a chance. To answer your question, the dead-end search warrants did figure into my decision. You guys tried to warn me." He shrugged. "I'm facing facts. The people in this town are more comfortable with its criminal element operating just under the radar. It seems everything is okay if it doesn't directly offend. As long as people support and accept wrongdoing, I'm wasting my time."

"What will you do?"

"Go back to my state job."

"Any chance you'll reconsider?"

Will gave a wistful smile. "No. I've already notified the governor."

Will left the barber shop. His announcement would spread over Sweet County like dandelion seed puffs in a stiff wind.

Back in the patrol car, Will unhooked the mic on his police radio and pressed the button to speak. "One to Sweet County."

"Go ahead, One," Pee Wee answered.

"This unit is 10-8."

"10-4. Good luck."

Fifteen minutes later, Will pulled off Highway 86 onto a dirt road. Scrub oaks and underbrush concealed the undercover agents' cars. Kirby Talkington and Winston Peel gathered around Sylvester, who sketched something in the sand.

"Drawing up battle plans?"

"Sort of." Sylvester pressed his hands against his thighs and straightened. "I was showing them my domain for the past couple of weeks."

Winston pulled up a photo on his phone screen and held it up. "Here's a shot of my latest buys. Liquor and marijuana are readily available from designated houses that take turns selling."

"I could buy hard drugs, even rainbow fentanyl," Kirby said, "but you have to deal discreetly. The influx at the border has found its way to Sweet County."

"Like I told you the other day," Sylvester said. "Your county is wide open. Pick your vice—booze, drugs, bolita—there is someone to oblige."

Will huffed. "No big surprise. I appreciate you going to the state attorney's office in Tallahassee with your reports and evidence yesterday."

"No problem. Your arrangement with the state attorney made it easy. Secretaries worked late and typed the affidavits and search warrants. Here you go."

Will accepted a large envelope from Winston and held it up like a victory medal. "My insurance against Judge Hallerton stonewalling me again."

"I'd like to be a bug on the wall when you hand the judge those warrants," Sylvester said.

Winston laughed. "Especially when he sees they're approved by State Attorney Dugan and only waiting for the judge's signature."

Will pulled a notebook from his front pocket. "I have lined up officers from agencies in close-by counties to be in each of your designated areas at five o'clock." He gave the men the names of the officers. "As soon as the judge signs the warrants, Tommy will deliver them, and you can start serving them immediately."

Will tapped the notebook with his pen. "For safe measure, I'll make it a point to have some questions to keep the judge tied up once Tommy has the warrants in hand. It's our turn to surprise them."

At four o'clock, Will placed a call to the judge's office. "Pam, could I speak to Judge Hallerton?"

"Hold on."

The judge's voice came on the line. "Sheriff. What's this I hear about you leaving us?"

Will smiled into the phone. Mission accomplished by the men at Bob's Barber Shop. "I've given the governor notice of my intentions, but I still have a few things for your input."

"The courthouse closes at five."

"I promise to be there by five, if you don't mind staying a little while."

"Why yes, I guess I could do that for you."

The five o'clock hour presented a quiet courthouse with darkened offices behind closed doors. The click of Will's and Tommy's heels echoed in the hall on the way to the judge's office.

Will rapped on the partially opened door of the judge's chambers.

"Come in."

Will entered, and Tommy stood behind him. Judge Hallerton, feet propped on his desk, ran a pocketknife under his fingernails.

The judge waved the knife. "Coffee grounds stuck under my nails. I should have had Pam take care of cleaning the coffeemaker before she left."

He swiped at the black bits he dug out and let them fall to the floor. This was surprising since he had been so meticulous about the neatness of the paperwork filed in his court.

Moving his legs off the desk, he clicked the blade closed and shoved the knife into his pocket. "Well, men, what do you have for me?"

Will turned to Tommy, who gave him a paper, and Will handed it to the judge. "I need your approval for this warrant."

The judge accepted the paper and adjusted his glasses. His brows creased together as he reached the bottom of the page. "This has been stamped and initialed already."

"Yes sir. The state attorney's office in Tallahassee drew these up for me. You're particular about your affidavits and warrants, and I wanted to be sure to have them in reasonable order before I brought them to you."

"Them?" Hallerton lurched forward in his chair. "What is this? You said you had a few things to run by me. How many?"

Will took the large clasp envelope from Tommy, which held the paperwork needed for the searches at locations where the undercover agents had made buys. "Just the ones in this envelope."

Judge Hallerton slid his glasses to the tip of his nose and glared. The man was backed into a corner. The fact that the state attorney who drew up the warrants was the same one who authorized the grand jury that indicted Sheriff Daly no doubt had registered with him.

"All the papers require is your signature."

Hallerton snatched the pen from its holder and scribbled his signature on the first paper, then pulled the stack from the envelope. He shook his head. "I know these people. I ... uh ... don't see them dealing in illegal substances. Who is this Winston Peel? Never heard of him."

"A beverage agent."

The judge dropped his head, and the overhead light reflected off a bald spot. He noisily scratched his signature on each page, then separated the affidavits from the warrants and shoved the stack toward Will.

"Does this mean you're not leaving?"

Thoughts of the argument with Annie swept over him. "I don't know, sir. I was sent to do a job." Will lifted the papers from the judge's desk, handed them to Tommy, and nodded for him to leave.

"If that's all you need from me ..." The judge placed his hands on the chair armrests and started to stand.

"Judge, from past experience, sometimes people won't open their door when we serve a warrant. Do you have a problem with us forcing a door open if we announce we have warrants?"

"As long as you identify yourself as the law and you have legal documents, you can use whatever force you deem necessary. But remember, these people have lived here all their lives. Don't use unnecessary force."

"I grew up in a small town. I understand. I assure you, we won't use undue force. When we pick them up, can they make bond right away, or do you prefer they appear before you?"

Hallerton ran his fingers through his graying strands of hair. "If you have to arrest anyone, book them as normal, but let them make an appearance bond at the next scheduled court date.

"Any evidence seized—"

The judge smacked his hands on the desk and stood. "Look, I appreciate your wanting to pick my brain, but I have to be somewhere, and handling evidence is not new to you."

"Of course. Sorry. I appreciate you taking the time to talk to me."

Outside the judge's office, Will checked his watch. He had detained the judge for twenty minutes.

Operation Clean Sweep was underway.

CHAPTER 25

She'd done it again—fired off words. And like bullets piercing a target, Annie couldn't take them back.

How could she fault Will for wanting a job he'd worked for and might lose? Didn't she have her own career dreams? She had to mend the rift between them before he left town.

Annie pulled into the sheriff's office parking lot with Jelly Bean at her side.

Nettie Sue had caught her just as she was leaving the parsonage. "Papa's having trouble catching his breath. The doctor said to take him to the clinic. Jelly Bean gets all out of sorts if he isn't fed at five-thirty."

Jelly Bean's ears had perked up at the "fed" word. Nettie Sue handed Annie a sack of food, his leash, and set his kennel on the porch. "I'll pick him up as soon as Papa is breathing better."

"I'll feed him, then I'm running to the sheriff's office. I'll take him with me, so if I'm not here when you come to pick him up, that's where we'll be."

She nodded and shuffled off the porch. The girl was thrifty with words. Annie could take lessons from Nettie Sue.

Putting the car in park, Annie retrieved the notebook on the back seat. As a peace offering, she'd compiled a correctly spelled list of common law enforcement terms used in legal documents. Rounding the car, she opened the passenger door. "Come on, boy. We need to make amends with Will."

Annie held the leash while Jelly Bean jumped from the seat and hit the ground on his stubby legs, shooting sand on her feet. Flip-flops were a poor choice of shoes while escorting a pig. She shook the sand from her shoes, then adjusted her Candy's apron. She'd been in such a rush to catch Will at work, she'd forgotten she had it on.

Inside, Pee Wee had the phone receiver wedged between his ear and shoulder while making a notation in the logbook.

"Yes, sir. I'll take care of it."

"Annie, hello. I see Nettie Sue has you pig-sitting again."

"Extemporaneous duty. Nettie Sue had to take her dad to the doctor and will probably pick up Jelly Bean here shortly."

"If you're here to see the sheriff, he's tied up right now. But I have a proposition I hope you won't refuse."

"Sure, if I can."

"Answer the phones for a few minutes. The sheriff ordered the holding cells freed up. I have to go release the pinkies." A grin crossed his face. "That's what we call the inmates who swear they'll never grace this jail again, thanks to your pink jail uniforms."

"Will is working? I thought—"

"That's an understatement." Pee Wee pushed back from his desk and stood. "I'll be back shortly."

Hope fluttered in Annie's chest, then came a flush of indignation. Had he changed his mind about leaving? If he did, why did he keep it from her? Annie placed the notebook for Will on the desk and unhooked Jelly Bean's leash.

"Jelly Bean, make yourself comfy. I intend to find out what's going on." The pig flopped down at her feet when the phone rang.

"Sheriff's office. Can I help you?"

"Uh ... I thought Pee Wee was on tonight."

"Tommy? It's Annie. Pee Wee asked me to fill in for a little while. Can I give him a message?"

"Just tell him the papers are delivered and radio transmissions will be limited for a while."

"10-4. Limited radio, papers delivered," she repeated and wrote in the logbook, noting the time. "He'll know what papers?"

"Sure, the warrants. I'll be 10-8."

Warrants? Plural. He had a bust going down and chose not to tell her? He said he was quitting and let her make a fool of herself with angry, impulsive accusations. She felt a heat push up her neck, remembering her tactless remarks. She had felt bad. But no more.

She slapped the notebook of commonly misspelled words she'd compiled for Will.

Jelly Bean jumped.

"Sorry, boy."

The entry door opened, and a man sauntered in wearing boots, jeans, and a western style shirt. A cowboy hat would have made his rancher look complete, but he wore a cap that anchored blond curls.

"Can I help you?"

The man wrinkled his forehead, slipped her a furtive glance, and looked over his shoulder. "I ... wanted to talk to the sheriff if he's in." He peered into Will's empty office. "But it don't look like he is."

The man surveyed the waiting area and hallway behind him. Sunshades hung by their arm from his shirt pocket. The glasses were the mirror type that had glared at her above a sinister sneer when her car was rammed off the road. Hairs prickled on the back of her neck.

"I'll use the restroom while I'm here."

Annie's insides tightened to rock. "This must be the guy," she whispered to Jelly Bean when the restroom door closed behind the man. Jelly Bean stood and snorted.

Annie hurried to the window. *Yes.* A white truck. She needed the tag number.

"Jelly Bean, stay." He sat back on his haunches.

Outside, Annie ran her hand over sticky residue on the truck's bumper where a sticker had been removed. She pulled the cell phone from her rear pocket and tapped the screen. Nothing. She tapped again and the home icons lit up. Hands trembling, she poked at the camera symbol and the phone flipped out of her hand, landing in the sand. "Great."

She stooped to retrieve it, but a boot shoved her fingers aside and ground the phone into the sand.

"Well." The hair-raising voice sliced through her. "Just as I thought." He produced the same sinister grin that had haunted her since being run off the road. "You are the law, working for the sheriff. I was right from the start."

"But ... What? I don't work here."

"You expect me to believe they just let anybody come in and answer phones at the sheriff's office? You're coming with me." He grabbed Annie by the arm and muscled her to the passenger door of the truck. "You may have other people fooled into thinking you're a waitress but not me. Get in."

"Are you crazy? I can't—"

He tightened his grip and opened the door. "Don't call me crazy. Get in."

His stare sent a wave of fear through her bones, making her knees go weak. He clasped both of her arms, lifted her, and shoved her onto the seat. One of her flip-flops fell off. He pushed the lock and slammed the door. A pack of Kool cigarettes slid off the dash, landing on the center console.

She had to get away. Pulse hammering, Annie pulled the lock and yanked on the door. The handle came off in her hand.

Will walked in the back door of the jail to the sound of chatter, laughter, and clinking glass bottles as Kirby shoved a case of whiskey into the corner of the evidence room. One of the beverage agents who came to assist with the one-night round up made a notation on a clipboard. The operation had been underway for an hour, and the office buzzed with activity.

"Howdy, Sheriff. Word is you quit today," Kirby said and winked.

"If you ever need to spread news, the local barber shop will do the trick. Who else is back?"

"Sylvester is booking a bolita operator. I believe he's in your office. We're spread out all over. Things have been hectic."

Will went out front where Pee Wee was hanging up the phone and writing in his log. "Hi, boss. Annie came by with Jelly Bean and left you this," he said, holding the notebook out to him.

"She left already?"

"Must have been in a hurry. When Nettie Sue arrived, she was miffed Annie had left Jelly Bean alone."

"That doesn't sound like Annie."

"I guess she figured the sheriff's office was as safe a place as any."

Will flipped the notebook open. The sight pricked a tender spot in his heart. Covered with letters of the alphabet, the front page read: *To spell proof your report and warrant writing. Wishing you success in your state job.*

Sylvester called out from the open door of his office. "Sheriff, I hope you don't mind me taking over your desk."

"No problem. I expect we'll use every inch of space around here before the evening's over." Will stepped inside his office. Rufus Tate sat in the guest chair. He grinned at Will. The gold cap on his front tooth glinted.

"Sir. You tol' me what you'd do, and you got me. But I has to tell you, I likes that you aren't rounding up just black folks. When I sees J.W. racin' out of here in his truck, I'm thinkin', yes siree, that sheriff is finally closin' in on the kingpin. You're gettin' white folks too."

"Are you talking about J.W. Evans?"

"Yes, sir. Drives that white truck and works at Redfern Farms. But I doubt I'm telling you somethin' you don't know."

Pee Wee walked in, scratching his head. "That's strange. I just noticed that Annie left her purse."

A sinking feeling wrenched Will's stomach. He pulled out his phone and called Annie. No answer.

"Rufus, show me exactly where you saw J.W.'s truck."

Rufus and Sylvester went to the grass and sand parking lot in front of the sheriff's office with Will.

Rufus pointed. "He was parked right there when I saw him back out." A flip-flop lay partially covered in sand.

Next to it was a cell phone, the face crushed. Will flipped the phone over.

A heaviness expanded in his chest, threatening to squeeze the breath out of him. The geometric design of the phone case told him the phone was Annie's.

He stashed the items in his jacket pocket.

"Could you see if anyone was with J.W.?"

Rufus's brows pushed together, and he rubbed the stubble on his chin. "I think so, but I only caught a glimpse. He was in a big hurry."

Will looked at Sylvester for an answer to the same question.

"I noticed the truck pulling out, but that's about it."

Will riveted his attention back on Rufus. "You said getting J.W. meant we were closing in on the kingpin. What did you mean?"

"I figured you were on to the whiskey sales racket."

"The racket has something to do with Redfern Farms?"

Rufus's forehead rolled up like a window shade. "Yes, sir ... I mean when I saw him—"

"Rufus, that farm is a big place. Do you know where they run the operation?"

His glance darted from Sylvester back to Will. "Understand that's not somethin' I deal in. Me, I'm a numbers man. So, all I know is what I heard."

A flush of adrenaline put every nerve in Will's body on alert. He had to find Annie. Right now, and Rufus was his best source of information. "No worries, Rufus. Gambling is all you're being charged with. What have you heard?"

"Well, sir, my friend Dilbert, who raises turkeys, was out near the Redfern farm cuttin' firewood and saw someone carrying a case of whiskey out of that big ol' metal warehouse. The building is down from the horse stables, kind of hid behind a stand of trees and surrounded by a barbed wire fence."

Tommy pulled into the parking lot in his patrol car and rolled down the window. "Sheriff. We caught 'em off guard. Your plan is working slick as a well-oiled gun. That judge is gonna' have a stroke."

"Do you still carry bolt cutters?" Will asked.

Puzzled, Tommy nodded to the rear of the car. "Yes, sir, in the trunk."

"Shotgun?"

"Yes, sir, but I swear I've been leavin' the turkeys alone."

Will motioned for Tommy to unlock his passenger door. "Sylvester," Will called over the roof of the car before climbing in. "Tell Pee Wee I'll be on the radio."

CHAPTER 26

Annie's throat squeezed tight, but she croaked out,"Wha—what do you think you're doing?"

"Hmpf." He cut his eyes toward her. "Like you don't know. You think we're just going to sit still while you people run roughshod over us?"

"You people?" Annie flung out her hands. "I don't know what you're talking about."

"Would you shut your trap?" He sped up and jerked the wheel erratically.

Should she grab the steering wheel? She was still banged up from the car wreck. The guy was big and driving too fast. She'd be no match for him.

His tires squealed as he took a corner. Annie had to brace herself with one hand on the dash. Three empty sugar packets clustered together with the tops torn off slid over and hit her hand.

"Slow down."

"I thought cops were big and brave. You sound like a wimp. You're confusing me."

"You're not the only one who's confused. Why do you insist I'm a cop, and why did you ram my car and run me off the road?"

"You followed us from Tallahassee."

"Us?"

"The horse trailer. I had to get you off our tail."

"I was going to Sugarville from Tallahassee. How else was I supposed to go?"

"Yeah. In Tallahassee at the governor's office, according to Uncle Al."

"Uncle Al? Is Al Redfern your uncle?"

He snickered. "Like that's a surprise. Art and Al are my mother's brothers. Look, I ain't stupid. The governor removed our sheriff and put in that other guy. That's when I saw I was right. You're a cop posing as a waitress at Candy's. My uncles eat there. The perfect place to snoop. I tried to tell them when you came nosing around the farm buying manure." His nostrils flared. "But they laughed at me. We'll see who gets the last laugh now."

That's where Annie had seen him. He helped his uncle with the carriage ride, and he retrieved the hand truck for Sandy at Redfern Farms. Sandy said his name, but she couldn't recall what it was.

Annie hadn't paid attention to the direction he was driving, only to his assertions. Though his crazy assumptions stemmed from wrong thinking, he had stumbled awfully close to the truth. To deal with this guy, she sensed staying calm and encouraging him to talk was the best strategy.

"What makes you say I was nosing around when I picked up manure and mulch at the farm? I needed the materials for my mother's rose garden."

"I heard you ask about bumper stickers and vehicles needing repair. The garden was an excuse in case anyone checked to see if you really needed manure and pine straw."

He tapped his chest. "I did check. And that's how I knew I'd get your attention, trampling the roses."

"You? Are you the one who hit me?"

"You shouldn't come to town and meddle in our business. I went to the sheriff's office tonight to see what was going on when I saw strangers handcuffing some of our distributors."

"Your distributors?" This guy glowed in self-pride. If she was trapped with him, she might as well take advantage of his cocky attitude and glean what she could. "You're big in the operation, I guess?"

"You have no idea."

"The next thing you're going to tell me is you were the one who left the note for me to go to the cabin."

He glanced at her, and a sneer crept across his face. "I instructed you to go alone. But you brought that sheriff with you. He's high on the get-rid-of list too."

Too? "He resigned as sheriff."

"Nah. Not after what I saw."

She didn't know what was in store for her, but she was on a roll. This guy loved to talk. "I suppose you know who killed other sheriffs who died mysteriously in this county?"

"Not only do I know, I know all the details."

"You're lying. When those sheriffs died you would have been a little kid."

"I'm not lying." Annie saw red splotches color his neck. He squinted and licked his lips. "My family members took them out."

"And you're bragging about it?"

His knuckles turned white, grasping the steering wheel. "Why not? You won't be around to tell."

Trees whizzed by barely visible in the darkness. He pulled up to a fence topped with barbed wire and punched in a number to open the electronic gate.

He drove through the gate and kept talking. "You stuck your nose in where you shouldn't. I tried to tell my uncles, but they brushed me off." He slapped the steering wheel. "Now we'll see what they say when they realize I was right."

He stopped abruptly behind a big metal warehouse. Annie pushed against the dash with her wrists to keep from toppling over.

Her accuser circled the truck and jerked the door open.

"Get out."

"Why?"

"'Cause I said so."

"So, you're the boss of me?"

Wrong question. He gripped her arm and hauled her out of the truck. His hand pressed into her back, steering her to the warehouse door. He pushed the door open and shoved her over the metal threshold. She stumbled and fell, scraping her knees again, this time against a concrete floor.

A roll-up door rumbled to a close at one end of the warehouse. She glimpsed a horse trailer loaded with boxes.

Two guys seated at a table in the center of the warehouse turned around. Annie recognized Sandy and Bubba.

Bubba swung his legs over the bench seat. "J. W., are you an idiot?"

J.W.? Now she had his name.

Sandy poked Bubba's back and chuckled. "Silly question." Sandy stood, hooking his thumb in a belt loop. "Why did you bring her here?"

J.W. kept a painful strangle hold on her arm and answered with an indignant, "She's a cop."

Sandy studied Annie. "Cop, huh? She fooled me."

"If I'm a cop, then you're the King of England," Annie said, stamping her foot and wrestling from J.W.'s grasp. "Has everyone gone bonkers around here?"

J. W. ignored her and asked, "Is all the whiskey out?"

"Loaded and on the move as we speak," Sandy said.

"Throw me that rope." J. W. signaled to Bubba.

Bubba shifted a lump in his mouth and spat out a long brown stream of liquid into a bucket sitting beside the table. "I checked her house and saw no evidence she's a cop."

The trio talked among themselves about her like she couldn't hear. Bubba reached for a rope hanging from a hook in the cavernous building filled with tall stacks of hay. The sweet, dusty odor coated her nose. She sneezed, sniffed, and wiped at her nose.

J.W. tramped up behind her, nudged her against a post and tied her wrists behind her. The coarse rope cut into her skin. Now her knees, nose, and wrists burned.

"She's been working undercover and knows way too much." J.W. said.

Sandy scowled at J.W.'s haughtiness. "Brilliant. And if she didn't know, she does now."

Sandy, a holstered gun at his side, walked over and eyed Annie as if she was a curiosity in a zoo. Skillfully, he maneuvered a piece of straw from one side of his mouth to the other, flipping it with his tongue. "She was asking a lot of questions when she was at the farm a couple of weeks ago."

Sandy, who'd been so kind and helpful with her garden order, had turned into a leering monster.

"And who was it that pointed it out to you?"

"Okay, J.W. Do you want a medal?"

J.W. lifted his chin and looked at her as if to say, "So there."

Bubba stood back as a spectator. He ran the back of his hand over the bulging wad of tobacco held in his cheek. The brown liquid oozed from the corner of his mouth.

The three lumbered over to the table and sat down. Bubba spit into a bale of hay this time instead of the bucket. J.W. hunched down on the table, resting on his forearms. "How do you propose we get rid of her?"

"Knock her out. Put her in her car and shove it into the ravine. It'll look like an accident," Bubba said.

"I was thinking of that, but no good," J.W. said. "Her car is sitting at the sheriff's office."

The scene was insane. "Are you guys out of your minds? You don't really think you can kill me and get away with it, do you?"

"You need to shut her up," Bubba said.

Sandy pulled an oily rag from his back pocket. "Here." He tossed it to J.W., and a laugh rumbled from his gut.

J.W. grabbed the rag.

"Okay, okay, so I'll be quiet while you plan my demise."

"And this will make sure you keep that promise." J.W. twisted the rag and pulled it between her teeth. Tying the oily cloth behind her head, the knot painfully yanked on strands of hair. The acrid smell shortened her breath, and the oil penetrated her tongue, making her gag. She could only manage short gasps to breathe.

"I need you quiet. I can't think with you babbling," J.W. muttered behind her.

Was this her legacy? Annie the burden and bother—even to her captors, making plans to do her in? She forced down a swallow of oil-tainted saliva and drew on the words of her dad's number two lecture. Prayer is your first line of defense.

The sky had turned from twilight to dark. While Tommy drove, Will tightened and released his fists. Scenarios ran through his head of what they might face—what Annie was facing.

He had formulated this plan to ensure complete secrecy for the raid. If he had let Annie in on the details of the operation, she wouldn't have felt compelled to make that notebook and bring it to the sheriff's office. And now she was in jeopardy.

Was J.W. Evans driving the white truck that ran Annie off the road? Who would ever think the guy who fought over a teddy bear at the fair could be capable of trying to harm Annie. And why?

J.W. had been right under his nose at the carriage ride. Will even had him in jail and let him go.

They couldn't reach Redfern Farms fast enough.

CHAPTER 27

Bubba flicked his thumb toward Annie. "J.W., you've created a problem for us, and I don't much appreciate it. When your uncles find out, they're gonna—"

"When your uncles find out what?" A voice boomed from the other side of the warehouse.

Art Redfern came into Annie's view.

"J.W. brought us a big surprise," Sandy said.

Art glanced her way. Bushy eyebrows lifted above widened eyes. He turned to glare at J.W.

J.W. clutched his hands on the table and whined, "But she recognized me, what else could I do?"

"You idiot." Art grabbed J.W. by the shoulder, forcing him to turn around. "How much does she know?"

J.W. shrugged his shoulders and cowered like he expected to be clobbered.

Bubba shifted his chew and spat into the bucket. "She saw the last load go out when J.W. brought her in."

"There's no telling what she knows," J.W. muttered. "She's a cop."

"Cop? What gave you that idea?" Art asked.

Bubba folded his arms over his paunch belly. "She ain't nothin' but a nosy waitress. I checked her house and purse.

No badge or credentials. Nothing to point to her being a cop."

"You expect her to advertise?" J. W. retorted. "She was working in the sheriff's office when I went in there."

Art gripped J.W.'s shirt collar, pulling him off his seat. "I told you to get a bead on what was going on at the sheriff's office. That's it."

"I did. And there's something going on."

"No kidding." Art turned J.W. loose with a shove so rough J.W. had to grab the side of the table to keep from falling.

Al stepped into Annie's view but did not make eye contact with her. "That sheriff supposedly quit, then we found out different when Hallerton called."

A combination of shock and disappointment washed over Annie. With his three-sugar-packet habit and quiet, caring demeanor, Al had seemed to be a sweet person. She would never have picked him to be involved in wrongdoing.

Bubba scrubbed the back of his hand over his tobacco-stained lips. "I should have taken out the Brice kid along with his mother twenty years ago."

Icy tentacles gripped Annie, traveling down her spine. Bubba shot Will's mother?

Al halted his pacing and pointed toward Bubba. "Don't even go there. If you had only fired a warning shot, as you were told, Finley Brice would have gotten the same message to keep his mouth shut. And whose idea was it to cut the brake lines and sabotage the sheriff's car?"

"Mine."

A woman's voice.

Shock was evident on three of the five faces in the barn as the woman came into Annie's view.

Bubba and Sandy stood. Dressed in black from her shoes to her cap with her long black hair threaded through the loop at the back, she appeared to be forty something, probably close to Sandy and Bubba's age. Whoever this woman was, she commanded deference that Art or Al did not appear to comprehend.

Art sputtered. "Why would you—"

Al interrupted Art. "Aren't you Judge Hallerton's secretary?"

"I am, but don't intend to be after tonight. You boys ready?"

In a swift choreographed move, the judge's secretary, Bubba, and Sandy each secured J.W., Art, and Al with plastic flex cuffs on their wrists and ankles like cowboys in a calf roping contest. Their move was so unexpected, they gave little resistance.

Art struggled to roll to his side. "Bubba. Sandy. I don't understand."

Bubba spoke as if tendering his resignation for a normal career move. "We've worked for you over twenty years. We kept your front operations going, handled your dirty work, and covered your whiskey operation."

"And we've paid you handsomely." Art said.

The judge's secretary stepped up. "Your operation brought in thousands. We found a way to make millions. After one last stop on the hill, we're set to fly out of here on our own jet, complete with pilot, to wherever we choose."

"What about her?" Sandy nodded in Annie's direction. "She's the waitress living at the parsonage."

Wishing she could shrink into the post she was attached to, Annie had hoped they might forget about her. No such luck.

The woman's eyes locked on her, then slowly scanned her like a copy machine preparing to send a fax. Her eyes narrowed. "Keep her tied up. Use the zip ties and bring her with us."

Bubba walked over, approaching her with the same indifference as he had gathering bales of pine straw. He made no eye contact. Roughly, he untied her from the post, kept the gag in place and bound her wrists behind her back with the flex cuffs. Her mouth salivated and drool dripped down the sides of her mouth. She wasn't sure which was worse, drooling or swallowing the oil leaching out of the dirty rag. She wished for more choices, but none materialized.

Sandy snickered and pointed at J.W. "He thought she was a cop."

"You wait and see." The concrete floor muffled J.W.'s shout.

"Wait? Our waiting days are over, pal. But not yours." Sandy had traded the piece of straw in his mouth for a cigarette. He took a long draw on it. The end glowed red. He tossed the cigarette into a bale of hay on the floor beside the three bound men. Smoke immediately rose from the dry straw.

Bubba jabbed Annie in the back, prodding her through the warehouse door. She looked back at the men writhing on the cement floor. A weight pressed inside her chest. How could they be so cruel, leaving them to burn to death?

Outside the warehouse, Annie's legs had trouble holding her up. She stumbled and lost her footing when a rock poked into the bottom of her shoeless foot. Bubba's rough grasp kept her from falling.

The secretary, who seemed to take the role of leader and decision maker, had teamed with Bubba and Sandy in a far more lucrative illegal business than the men they had tied up like sausages and left to roast. Her three captors might not realize she was an undercover agent but were well aware that she knew too much.

She not only had the name of the guy who ran her off the road but who had been in her house and shot Will's mother.

Bad guys and even badder guys existed in Sweet County, and these three qualified for the latter. Neither Bubba nor the woman flinched when Sandy flicked the cigarette into the hay. They exhibited zero concern over leaving three men tied and helpless in a barn destined to go up in flames.

Bubba steered her toward a black Escalade.

What did they intend to do with her?

She twisted her hands against the restraining cuffs. Her efforts burned and bit painfully into her wrists. But doing nothing was not an option. She had to do something.

Lord, all ideas are welcome.

Her hands dropped to her low back and rested on the knot of her Candy's Café apron. She felt below the knot and tugged on the wide cloth sash. The fabric tie loosened.

Bubba opened the rear door. "Get in."

Bubba placed his hand above her head, guiding her under the door frame. *Nice.* He'd keep her from bumping her head but not hesitate to bump her off.

As she bent down to climb into the car, Annie gave the apron sash a swift tug. The long stretch of tie released and caught in the door when he closed it. *Yes.* Someone might notice the tie hanging out and realize something was wrong.

Bubba opened the door behind the driver and sat beside her. The woman started the car.

"Pam, why are we taking her along?" Sandy asked sliding into the front passenger seat.

Pam. She had her name.

"Insurance. Having her with us will prevent them from using lethal force. We'll pick up the last drug shipment and hightail it out of here. Once we're on the plane and flying over the Gulf, we can unload her."

She looked in the rearview mirror and spoke to Bubba. "Secure her legs."

Bubba had a ready supply of cuffs. He wrapped her ankles and pulled the heavy plastic bands tight.

Just as Rufus had described, cedar trees shrouded the warehouse on Redfern Farms behind a six-foot fence topped with two feet of barbed wire. A utility light glowed above a watering trough and the open door at the rear of the building. Beside the door, a white pickup sat with the passenger door ajar.

"What now, boss?" Tommy asked Will.

"Cut into the fence. We're going in."

"Will do."

Tommy retrieved his bolt cutters from the trunk. He snapped the fence wire with his powerful hands and bent back an opening.

Will squeezed through, ignoring the jagged edges of the wire biting at his clothes and arm. He adjusted the gun and holster on his side, and Tommy shoved his way through behind him. Scrambling past the truck, Will heard voices and squatted behind the watering trough. Smoke clouded the door opening.

Tommy knelt beside Will.

"I'm going in. Back me up." Will drew his gun and stepped inside the hazy interior. Keeping his back to the wall, he quickly surveyed the area. Behind a veil of smoke, three men bound at the wrists and ankles lay struggling against their restraints on the floor. Smoke billowed from the hay beside them, making Will's eyes water. There was no sign of Annie. The men cursed and coughed. Suddenly, flames shot up from one of the hay bales as fire took hold.

Will holstered his gun and turned to Tommy, who remained close behind him.

"Hand me the bolt cutters. There's a water hose outside. Try to stop the fire from spreading."

A flame leaped from one bale to a short stack close to the men's heads.

Amid terror-stricken expletives, Will recognized the twin profiles of Al and Art Redfern and the panicked voice of J.W. Evans.

Will rushed to them. "Hold still. I'll free your ankles first."

"We're gonna burn!" J.W wailed.

"Hush, J.W." Art twisted around on one shoulder. "Thank God, Sheriff. Get us out of here."

Tommy blasted the fire with the water hose. The burning hay hissed, sending up black smoke. The acrid smell filled the building, making it hard to breathe.

"Oh, God. Oh, God." J.W. bucked and kicked. "We're gonna die!"

"It's going to be okay," Al said in a calming tone. "The sheriff needs you to be still to free your ankles."

The hay crackled, steam spewed, and the spiraling smoke coated Will's nostrils and throat. Through blurred vision, Will pressed against J.W.'s legs, feeling for the restraints. Finding them, he worked the cutters into place and pressed hard. The heavy plastic strap snapped.

"Go outside while I free your uncles." J. W. stood and started to the door. He lost his footing and tumbled to the floor.

Will quickly cut Art and Al's ankle restraints. The men grabbed J.W. and scrambled outside, coughing and grumbling.

Tommy continued dousing the last of the flames.

"Good work, Tommy."

"Thanks. If the flames had reached that tower of hay bales stacked to the ceiling, the fire would have been impossible to stop. I'll make sure it's soaked real good."

Outside, J.W. bent over, hands on knees, coughing. Al patted his back.

Will wiped his face, wet from sweat and watering eyes. "J.W., where's Annie?"

J.W. looked up, his dirt-smudged face twisted in a childlike pout. "I don't know."

Will grasped J.W.'s shirt collar at the neck.

Mucus from his nose, made a dirt trail into his mouth. "Sandy, Bubba. They took her," J. W. whined.

"He's telling the truth," Al said. "Sandy, Bubba, and Pam Reston took Annie with them."

"Pam? The judge's secretary?"

"Yes." Al lifted his bound hands, surrender style. "I confess we've been dealing in illegal whiskey sales. But the three who took Annie are involved in something I swear we are not a part of."

Art chimed in. "Pam talked about making millions and said they'd make a last stop on the hill before taking a jet out of here."

"The hill?"

"The Fleming house, turned parsonage, that sits on a hill," J.W. said, keeping his eyes on his shoes. "I overheard Bubba and Sandy talking about storing stuff in that old house cause it stood empty for a long time."

Tommy came outside. "Fire's out."

"Tommy, stay here and toss me your car keys."

Tommy complied, and Will snatched the keys out of the air.

While hustling to the patrol car, he used his cell phone to contact the sheriff's office. "Pee Wee, send the team working the west side to meet Tommy at Redfern Farms and pick up three subjects. Have the east side team put a hold on whatever they're doing and meet me at the parsonage on Sugar Avenue, ASAP."

CHAPTER 28

Pam drove carefully, not exceeding the speed limit. Only one car met them before reaching Sugarville's city limits, where Pam turned onto Sugar Avenue. They drove past Lessie and Jessie's Sweet Nothin's Hair and Wear and the courthouse. The deserted streets left no one to see her sash hanging from the car.

Pam drove out of town on Sugar Avenue. When she neared Community Church, she turned off the headlights and pulled in behind the church. The house on the hill stood as a dark, austere sentinel with only the light of the full moon reflecting off its windows.

Pam issued new instructions. "The last shipment of fentanyl is boxed. Set it outside the basement first, then we'll form a chain to hand out the remaining bundles."

They had a stash in the parsonage basement? Where? The lighting was poor in the cellar, but the space only held wooden shelves with canning jars, an old chair, and her rat trap.

The men nodded. All three wordlessly left the car. The doors locked with a click.

The three slipped into the shadows, making their way up the hill to the side of the house with the basement door.

But instead of going down the steps to the basement, they tromped through the damaged rose garden to the trellis. Detail was hard to make out in the moonlight, but they slowly disappeared behind the trellis.

A hidden door or window? Annie leaned forward, straining to see. The seatbelt held her back. She dropped her head against the seat rest and a flash of comfort washed over. Like a light set to come on at dark, she was nudged with the assurance of her Mom and Dad's continual prayers for protection over her.

Lord, I praise you for answered prayer in my life, and right now I could use your help big time. I'm fresh out of ideas.

She'd been in tight spots working undercover before. Like the time she feigned stomach cramps and escaped from a bathroom window.

Think. Look around you.

She sat up, mind racing. Was there something she should see? A way out of the cuffs? The binding on her ankles and wrists only tightened and bit in harder as she tugged. *Think.* She could move her feet and wiggle her toes unhindered.

Her eyes searched. Was there anything useful she could access? On the door? The floorboard? The console between the front seats? Then she saw it, glinting in the moonlight.

Will blasted past the 45-mph speed limit sign, going eighty. Wrong place, wrong time ... again. Failure pressed hard against his chest. He'd unknowingly failed his mother by changing his after-school plans and failed Annie by keeping plans from her. If he'd shared the sting operation with Annie, she wouldn't be in danger now. He played the plan close to the vest and hoped to surprise the illegal operators and impress the higher ups, along with Annie. *Reprehensible.*

Entering Sugarville from Cookie Street, Will braked and made a tire smoking turn onto Sugar Avenue. Gus's brake repair job held. He sped past the businesses on the square. The burgundy and pink-striped awnings rippling in the breeze displayed sweetness, but many facades in Sweet County concealed unsavory behaviors and culprits. Like the three who took Annie.

Lord, please keep Annie safe.

He slowed when he neared the parsonage and radioed the west side car, cautioning them not to use lights or siren. He cut his lights before passing the church and eased into the drive, stopping beside the lion statues. But he was not the first one there.

He recognized Nettie Sue's blue truck with the *I Love Pigs* bumper sticker. She was turning off her headlights and had the driver's door open when Jelly Bean leaped out, thudding to the ground on all fours. He sniffed the air and took off toward the ruined rose garden.

"Jelly Bean!" Nettie Sue hollered.

So much for a quiet entrance.

Jelly Bean kept going, and Will rushed to Nettie Sue, shushing her with his index finger to his lips. "Please, it's important you remain quiet and stay here. I'll retrieve Jelly Bean."

A pig gone wild confronted Will when he rounded the corner of the house. Jelly Bean bucked and snorted with sharp, grating grunts, kicking up leaves and pine needles in the ravaged rose garden that held the memory of Will and Annie's kiss.

Hang professionalism. Lord, please let me have the chance to hold Annie again.

Hearing a man's voice, Will remained in the shadows.

"Hey. There's a pig out here." Bubba emerged from a basement window and flung a sack to the ground, landing next to other packages wrapped in heavy plastic. Judging from Jelly Bean's contortions, the packages contained drugs. The rose trellis, attached to a hinged piece of siding, blended with the house, cleverly concealing a secret entry.

Sandy peered out of the basement access. "Oh, that kind of pig. You scared me. I thought you were talking about the kind that wears a badge."

"There's somthin' funny going on. The pig looks like Jelly Bean, and he's gone crazy," Bubba said.

Sandy climbed out of the basement, followed by Pam, each carrying bundles in their arms.

"What's crazy is naming pigs," Pam said. "Grab that stuff and let's go."

Only three came out of the basement. Where was Annie? With no time to wait for backup or to devise a plan, Will had to act.

Stepping from the shadows into a strip of moonlight, he trained his 9mm on them. "You've earned both kinds of pigs. Hands up against the wall and spread your legs."

"Oh, man." Sandy said, dropping his package.

Sandy and Bubba followed directions with hands pressed against the wall. But as soon as Pam touched the wall, she pushed back and bolted down the hill.

The chirp of a car unlocking came from the shadows behind the church.

Behind him a beam of light lit up a black car at the foot of the hill. A piece of pink fabric was caught in the door. Annie?

"Sheriff, you need light out here," Nettie Sue said matter-of-factly, sweeping the light around the area. Pam disappeared into the shadows on the other side of the black car. Both Sandy and Bubba jumped away from the wall and started down the hill. Where was backup?

Suddenly, Jelly Bean snorted and lunged at Sandy, knocking him off his feet with a block that would make any defensive coach proud. Sandy cartwheeled in the air and did a four-point landing into the thorny pile of rose bush remains. Jelly Bean hopped on his back and Sandy yowled.

Will caught up with Bubba and tackled him at the ankles. They both thudded to the ground. Will slapped handcuffs on his wrists.

Nettie Sue held her high beam flashlight in one hand and shotgun in the other. "I got 'em, Sheriff. Don't neither one of you move."

"Don't worry. I can't move with this fool pig on my back," Sandy grumbled.

A female scream came from the car. Fear shot through Will. He dashed down the hill. Hitting a slick spot, he lost his footing and slid on rocky rubble, his elbow digging into the dirt. The car engine revved. He couldn't let her get away. Pushing off the ground, Will reached for his pistol and fired at the black car's front tire, point blank. The blast sent a shock wave to his eardrums. He ran toward the screams, now muffled in his ringing ears, and slammed into someone's back.

He barely made out Pam's shouted words. "Let go. You're gonna break my arm."

The driver's door stood open with Pam behind the steering wheel struggling to free her forearm pinned to the door frame. She clawed at the man's long hair with her other hand.

"Shag?"

"Yes, sir. Holding this one for you."

"Let me out of here and take this thing off my back," Pam yelled. Will trained his gun on Pam, opened the door, and motioned for her to step out. "Hands up where I can see them."

"They're up. My shoulder. Get if off me."

Stuck to her shoulder like a pinup on a bulletin board was a flip-flop. He tugged it loose. Sticking from the bottom of the shoe like a cleat was the sharp point of the pin-back clasp of a "Sweet as Pie" button.

Kirby ran up behind Will, breathless. "Sorry it took so long, Sheriff. I'll do the honors." He slapped handcuffs on Pam's wrists.

While she moaned and muttered obscenities, Will heard muted sounds coming from the back seat. Annie. His insides quivering, Will hit the unlock button, rushed to the rear door where he'd seen the pink sash. Pulling the door open, thanks washed over him at a sight more lovely than the grandest sunset in God's creation—Annie—hair mussed, eyes wide, and muttering unintelligibly.

"Annie, are you okay?"

She nodded vigorously and turned her head so the knot holding the gag in place faced him. He yanked it loose, pulling the rag from her mouth.

She worked her jaw from side to side. "Thank you, Lord in heaven. Will," she nodded toward Pam being led away. "She's a drug dealer and stashed drugs in the parsonage. Did you see Jelly Bean. Wasn't he something?"

"Yes, and I saw the weapon you somehow fashioned with your shoe."

"The Redferns are involved—"

"There will be plenty of time to talk. Hold still." Will pulled out his pocketknife and cut her restraints. From the looks of her raw, red wrists, she'd endured pain at the hands of her captors. She flung her freed arms around his neck in a sweet hug and warm tingles shot over him to match the ringing still in his ears from firing the gun.

In seconds, a flurry of activity flooded the property. Two unmarked state cars had pulled in with the beverage agents. Car headlights lit the area. Bubba, Sandy, and Pam were all taken into custody.

"J.W. ran me off the road ... part of the basement is hidden ... Jelly Bean acting crazy in the living room makes sense now ..."

Will guided her away from the work of the lawmen to a bench seat under a tree behind the church. He'd so feared his failings had brought disaster to Annie and he'd lost her forever. Just the taste of life without her had sickened him.

Annie continued to talk in one continuous stream. Then, stopping to take a breath, she lifted her chin and stared at him a moment with sweet brown eyes that gradually squinted. "Wait a minute." She poked him in the chest. "You lied to me."

"What?"

"You didn't really quit."

"For the bust to have any hope of success, I had to have my resignation look real."

She sat up ramrod straight. "We were supposed to be working together."

"You had a concussion."

"I was getting better."

"I realized that when you scorched me with fiery darts about my father."

"I ... well ..." Annie's face turned fuchsia. "I warned you about my impulsive behavior." Annie wagged her index finger at him. "Besides, I thought better of my misspoken words. That's why I made you a notebook, to show you I understood your decision to leave."

He studied her pouting face. When had this independent, smart, and sometimes exasperating woman taken a foothold in his heart?

She poked him in the chest again. He locked his gaze on the moonlit glint in her eyes. Her voice squeaked out an octave higher. "Still, you didn't trust me—"

Will cupped her face in his hands. "Can we sort out all your complaints later?"

"Well ... maybe. She hooked her mussed hair behind her ears. "Did you have something else in mind?"

"I do. With the success of this raid tonight, I'm ready to untuck those personal feelings we talked about ... if it's okay."

Annie reached up and cradled his face in her hands. "Will Brice, untuck away."

Drawing her close, their lips met, unraveling the fears and dissolving the tensions of the chaotic night. She slipped her arms around his neck and responded to his kiss with a slight, pleasurable sigh, stirring a praise of thanks to the Lord for having Annie safe in his arms.

Something nudged Will's leg.

Will broke off the kiss and looked down.

Jelly Bean pushed between their feet, sat down, and grunted.

"Jelly Bean don't like loud talkin'," Nettie Sue said, peering down at them.

Will absorbed the rebuke in Nettie Sue's eyes and the forlorn look in Jelly Bean's, staring back at him.

Annie stooped down and patted Jelly Bean. "It's okay, buddy. Just an intense discussion and we made up already."

Will rested his hand on Annie's and gave it a gentle squeeze. Then, he leaned down and patted the coarse hair on the pig's head. "She's right, Jelly Bean, just a discussion. I'm ready to deputize you." He looked up at Nettie Sue, still holding the flashlight and cradling her shotgun in the crook of her arm. "Both of you."

Nettie Sue returned a non-expression. "Not necessary." She lifted her non-gun-toting shoulder in a shrug. "Glad to help. I just come for Jelly Bean's kennel."

CHAPTER 29

Four weeks later

Annie stood at the top of the porch steps of the parsonage. A pang of uncertainty shot through her heart as Will pulled into the drive. Would this be one of his last official days as sheriff? Governor Renfroe had made certain Will's certification waiver was approved with FDLE. He could return to his state job any time, and the governor would name a new appointee. Was that the direction God would have him go?

Annie had danced a jig when Craig Dillavey offered her the job she'd interviewed and prayed for. The offer was an open door. Yet, now watching Will climb the steps, was that what she wanted? More importantly, was that the direction God desired for her?

When he reached the porch, he touched her hands and examined her wrists. Only a faint redness remained.

"Bad news."

"Why bad news?"

"After four weeks, you can barely see that you were a kidnap victim. I no longer have an excuse to check on you every day."

"You need an excuse?"

He cocked his head and raised a brow. "We are under the scrutiny of Sweet County."

She gave a surrendering tilt to her head and chuckled. "You speak the truth. I'm glad to have this time alone before the downtown event."

"Do you have any idea what the mayor has arranged?"

"Not exactly." Annie resisted the urge to touch the cute cleft indention in his chin and opted to kiss his cheek instead. "But I suspect it will have something to do with Sheriff Brice netting twenty-three arrests during his undercover raid in Sweet County, which drew praise from the governor."

"Or maybe he will extol the town pig and waitress who snared the drug traffickers and kidnappers."

"Whatever is planned, we have thirty minutes before we have to report to the town square. Let's sit down." Annie took Will's hand.

"At this point, I'm glad to follow someone else's orders instead of issuing my own."

Will sat beside her on the porch swing. The touch of his shoulder and breathing in Will's clean sandalwood scent sent a tingling awareness through her. "Since the raid, each day sheds more light on the graft in this town."

"You're right. I'm still piecing motives and actions together."

"I am astounded that just because J.W. thought I was a law enforcement officer he would try to run me down and shoot me. Crazy."

"I believe he viewed the task as a kind of family mandate. Al Redfern said J.W. is intellectually challenged, and he and Art had kept J.W. employed with jobs around the farm over the years. He was supposed to be a lookout for his uncles' illegal whiskey operation, but his ego and self-pride took over. J.W. believed running you off the road, shooting at you, and trampling the rose garden would scare you off ... and win favor for him in his family's eyes. Years of being made the brunt of jokes made him more determined. He wanted to be a big man and contribute."

"Too bad he'll never know how close he came to the truth."

Will slipped his arm around Annie and patted her shoulder. "Yes, and I was privileged to witness Mary Hart in action firsthand. The night of the raid, Shag became suspicious when he saw the pink sash caught in the car door, waving like a flag. When the car's lights went out and pulled behind the church, he followed. But the clincher," Will removed his arm from her shoulder and turned to her, eyes dancing, "was stopping Pam Reston in her tracks with your Sweet as Pie shoe spike. The McAfee, perfectly placed, double-footed karate jab to the shoulder ..." He smacked his hands together with a loud pop. "... is now legendary. Little wonder FDLE wants to continue tapping into their Mary Hart secret weapon when needed."

Annie laughed and leaned back in the swing and sent it swaying. "I credit the good Lord for dropping those ideas on me. But tell me the truth. Was Al really a part of the illegal whiskey ring?"

"He was, but I believe he hated being involved. He and Art inherited the three-generations-old Redfern Farms with its legitimate farm equipment and horse business, but the lucrative illegal whiskey trade was also embedded in that inheritance."

Annie clicked her tongue. "Pity. He was always such a nice, courteous man at the café."

"Don't forget, Al is the one who slipped you the cash with a warning."

"He must have suspected J.W. right away and tried to protect him."

"Al also admitted his wife wrote the 'stop' note. Since their son, Clint, had been questioned in Adam's death, she feared your research of underage drinking would stir up trouble they did not want to face."

Annie drew in a breath and gave a reluctant nod of acceptance. "The Redfern brothers continued to employ Bubba and cover for him, knowing he killed your mother."

"Bubba swears her shooting was an unintended accident. His intentions and confession bring closure but will never replace the years I've missed with my mother ... and by extension, my father."

"Sorry to bring up that past hurt."

Will leaned forward, clasped his hands between his knees. "No need to apologize. This appointment as sheriff has disrupted my career but forced me to confront the pain from my past. My father finally explained he'd gone to Redfern Farms to purchase farm equipment and inadvertently witnessed the organized crime operation. He'd agreed to testify, but after mother was shot, they threatened to take my life if he didn't back off."

Will snorted. "All this time, I attributed his tension to blaming me for my mother's death. But instead, he feared for my life and felt the best safeguard for me was to become self-sufficient and leave the area."

"Why didn't your dad just pack you up and move?"

"The land. Like the Redferns, the farm had been handed down to my father. Farming is in his blood. If he sold, he could never replace the sweat equity he and my ancestors had in the land."

Annie rested her hand on Will's shoulder. "And Bubba, who committed felonies, also played games by adding laxative to weed brownies?"

"J.W. claims Bubba came up with the tainted brownies idea as payback to the Becks over the teddy bear incident. Bubba wanted to see what happened at the golf course. J.W. went with him and witnessed Bubba and Adam get into a scuffle—which accounts for Bubba's boot print at the scene—but says Adam was standing and hollering at them when they drove off. Bubba may not have drowned Adam, but he is indirectly responsible."

"What happens next?"

"Since Art, Al, and J.W. pled guilty to charges and are awaiting sentencing, I will concentrate on furnishing evidence for the prosecution of Bubba, Sandy, and Pam."

"Put Jelly Bean on your witness list." Annie chuckled. "We know now what made him act crazy in the living room. He sniffed out the drug stash in the secret cellar."

"Which led to the discovery of the trap door under the carpet runner in the living room where Bubba accessed the house."

"Rats, big ones, were in the basement after all."

"Yup. And two of the rats have been ratting on Pam to anyone who will listen. She arrived in town with midlevel drug smuggling connections. When she became aware of the illegal transport of whiskey into the county, she smelled the opportunity to team up drug trade with the operation already in place and dangled the carrot in front of Bubba and Sandy."

"Money creates interesting matchups. I was surprised to learn Pam lived here in the parsonage for a short time after her uncle inherited the house."

"According to Sandy, her full name is Pam Fleming Reston, and she discovered the trapdoor where old man Fleming kept his moonshine still. Stirring haunted house rumors gave them a perfect cover for the clandestine drug operation she contrived until her uncle decided to sell to the church."

"There is no doubt Pam was the mastermind." The memory of Pam's sinister voice spewing orders still knotted Annie's stomach and shot painful sensations to her wrists and ankles. "She was a mean woman."

Shaking off the thought, Annie pushed forward on the swing. "We should probably head downtown." She automatically reached for her phone to check the time and snapped her fingers. "I forgot. I left my phone at Candy's. What time is it?"

"We have a few minutes." Will reached to clasp her hand. "But before we go, I need to tell you something."

"Yes?"

"With the flurry of dealing with the prisoners and hearings, all while running the department with a skeleton crew, I—" His phone sounded. "Sorry."

Annie heard Tommy's voice when Will answered the phone.

"Boss, people are waiting for you downtown. Where are you?"

Five minutes later, Annie and Will pulled onto Confection Street. Cars clogged the downtown area. A crowd had gathered on the courthouse lawn in front of the gazebo, while others crowded the sidewalks. Many of the merchants had set up tables with "Appreciation Day Specials."

Candy had a dispenser of water with fresh lemon slices outside the café. Across the square, Jessie and Lessie sold special gift baskets filled with hair accessories and sewing supplies.

Tommy waved them into a space reserved with an orange cone. "Sheriff, I think the whole county turned out. Pee Wee and I had to make the street one way to create an extra parking lane."

"Good thinking." Will parked, and when he stepped from the car, clapping started. Will rounded the car and opened her door. Applause worked its way through the crowd until cheers erupted among the entire gathering. A sign hanging above the gazebo read—*We Appreciate Sheriff Brice.*

Mayor Fox took his place behind the speakers' stand in the gazebo and coaxed the audience to move in closer. Winnie met them and steered Annie and Will forward through the throng that parted to let them pass. Familiar faces dotted the crowd. Among them were Police Chief Woodham, Bob Kittrell from the barber shop, Rex from the corner gas station, and Sidney Burrell and Royce Tinsley from the country club. Lessie and Jessie waved enthusiastically. Shag stood nearby with a press camera around his neck and pad and pencil in hand.

In front of the gazebo, Winnie placed Will and Annie beside Nettie Sue and Jelly Bean, who was wearing a bright red bandanna with a matching red collar and leash.

The mayor tapped the microphone, testing the sound.

"Sheriff Brice ..." The microphone squealed. Jelly Bean shrieked, and Nettie Sue covered his ears. The mayor motioned to the man handling the PA system and tried again.

"Sheriff Brice, I have been appointed to make this proclamation." He opened a rolled document, cleared his throat, and read.

"Whereas the grateful citizens of Sweet County express their appreciation and recognize Will Brice for his dedication and unwavering devotion to law enforcement as Sheriff of Sweet County, Florida, we the undersigned respectfully request that he remain in the Office of Sweet County Sheriff and fulfill his appointment by the Governor of the State of Florida until the next scheduled election."

Applause broke out among the spectators.

"If you'll stay, I'll toss in a free bucket of used golf balls on Monday afternoons," Sidney Burnell yelled.

"Speech," Bob Kittrell called out.

Winnie raised her hand. "Hold up. The mayor is not finished."

Mayor Fox read from another paper. "Annie McAfee, with your expertise and the information materials you designed to warn our young people about the dangers of drug abuse, we of the city council collaborated with the county commission to offer you the public relations job for the Sweet County Chamber of Commerce."

Annie's mouth dropped. They were offering her a job in Sweet County after the controversy she'd stirred?

Cora Neddles spoke up. "Mayor, I taught you in senior English, and I'm surprised you're so smart."

Jelly Bean grunted.

Laughter rippled among those who heard. "Even the town pig agrees," Cora shouted.

The mayor beamed. "I'm honored for the commendation. Nettie Sue, bring Jelly Bean up here. Sheriff, you and Annie come up too."

Nettie Sue led the way. Jelly Bean's hooves clomped loudly on the wooden steps and echoed across the platform leading to the lectern.

The mayor read from another paper and held up a blue ribbon for the crowd to see. "Jelly Bean, whereas you were instrumental in the sniffing out and capture of criminals who were a threat to Sweet County, as mayor, I hereby bestow on you the title of Sugarville Super Swine. And to Nettie Sue Forehand, his trainer, it is my great pleasure to offer heartfelt thanks and a space at the city hall to display and sell your crafts."

Mayor Fox shook Nettie Sue's hand and stooped down to hang the ribbon around Jelly Bean's neck. Jelly Bean snorted and sat back on his haunches. The audience cheered, and this time the loud noise didn't seem to bother Jelly Bean at all.

Handing Will the official proclamation and Annie the public relations job offer, Mayor Fox shook their hands. "Folks, for the rest of the day, join in the downtown fun. We have jumping inflatables on the other side of the courthouse for the kids and merchants are offering specials all around the square. Enjoy."

After more applause, Shag cornered Nettie Sue and Jelly Bean for photos, and the crowd began to scatter.

The mayor guided Annie and Will to the side. "I know both of you have other job opportunities, but I hope you will give our proposals some serious thought."

"I'm surprised you want me to stay after I disrupted the status quo," Will said.

"No surprise to me." The voice came from behind them. "The citizens seem to love you."

Will turned. His eyes lit up in surprise. "Dad." Will wrapped his arm around his father's shoulder. "Mayor Fox, my father, Finley Brice. He lives in Summit City in Hill County."

"Great place. I believe the Summit City mayor is here. Have you met him?" he asked Will's father.

"No, sir. I've only seen him on the local news."

The resemblance of Will to his father was unmistakable. Though his was gray-streaked, his father had the same auburn colored hair, solid build, and the cleft chin Annie adored on Will.

Patting Will on the shoulder, the mayor said, "You must be proud of this fine boy you raised." Someone tugged on the mayor's sleeve. "If you'll excuse me."

"The mayor is right, I am proud. But I'm ashamed to say my backing away allowed the crime here to continue for years."

"You did what you thought best at the time," Will said.

"Protecting you drove my decisions."

Annie spoke up. "I believe this was the appointed time to clean up the corruption. Mr. Brice, you played an important part by keeping Will safe until now."

Will took Annie's hand. "Dad, meet Annie McAfee. She heroically helped bring the criminals to justice."

"Finley." Mayor Fox called out and motioned for Will's dad to join him. "Here's the mayor I want you to meet."

His father made kind remarks to Annie and excused himself when Candy rushed up, waving Annie's phone. "Annie, your phone beeped. When I saw it was a text from your parents, I knew you would want to see it right away."

Annie's heartbeat ratcheted up. "Oh dear, I hope nothing has happened to Mom and Dad." She pulled up the message. Her heart calmed, but her mouth went slack.

Will touched her shoulder. "Is everything okay?"

She looked up at Candy and Will's concerned faces. "Listen to this." She read out loud. "Heard from Reverend Sewell about your heroic stand to help clean up Sweet County. Proud of you. Be home soon. Love Mom and Dad."

"Proud of me." She prodded herself in the chest with her thumb. "Imagine. My folks have been pleased and appreciative, but never proud."

"Well, they should be proud 'cause you are a special person and a pretty good waitress too." Candy winked. "Enjoy the rest of the day, but I need you for the breakfast shift in the morning." Candy hurried back across the street.

"Think of it," Annie said, holding up the text for Will to see. "You and I both have proud parents, and we each have two job offers."

"The Sweet County Chamber would be lucky to have you."

"You really think so?"

"Yes, I really think so."

Will's gaze made her knees go rubbery. What would it be like to stay in Sweet County—with Will? A dull ache touched her heart. Both had their dream futures waiting for them. But those jobs would take them away from Sweet County ... and each other.

"Odd as it may seem," Will said, "if I take the state job and leave, I'd miss Sweet County."

"*If* you leave?"

Will nodded, pursing his lips. "And I'd miss living near my father, who I've just reconnected with."

"I'd miss being near my parents who just moved here."

Will took Annie's hands and placed them on his shoulders, then positioned his hands at her waist. "I'd miss their meddlesome daughter."

Annie clasped her hands behind Will's neck. "I'd miss skirting around your directives."

Will ran his fingers over her cheek and around the outline of her lips. An electrifying tingle washed over her. "I'd miss pink jail uniforms."

"I'd miss shooting lessons." She touched her finger at the rim of his ear.

"Annie, all I know ..."

Something bumped her leg, breaking the delicious spell. Jelly Bean flopped down, covering both Annie's and Will's feet.

Nettie Sue walked over, winding up a paper streamer and placed it in a bag. "Jelly Bean got tired of following me around. I plan to make confetti from these decorations. No need lettin' them go to waste. Go ahead doin' what you're doin'." She gathered another strip of crepe paper and walked away, rolling it up.

Jelly Bean grunted. The blue ribbon rested on his crossed front hooves.

Will lifted his eyes heavenward.

Annie tugged on his hands. "You were saying, 'All I know ...'" she prompted.

He gently lifted her hands to his chest. "All I know is I've grown to care for you and find the idea of being where you're not too ..." he glanced at Jelly Bean. "... dismaying."

"I'll stay if you stay," Annie blurted.

"You stole my line."

"Impulse."

"Marry me?"

Annie gulped. "Seriously?"

Jelly Bean uttered a soft snort.

"Your impulsivity is catching," Will smiled coyly.

With that, Annie grabbed his shirt collar, pulled his head down and kissed him square on the lips. Will drew her close and deepened the kiss.

Annie snuggled into his embrace.

She relished the sense of acceptance and belonging from her parents and the townspeople. But most of all, she savored the love of the man holding her. Warm ... cozy ... sweet.

ABOUT THE AUTHOR

Sally Jo Pitts brings a career as a private investigator, high school guidance counselor, and teacher of family and consumer sciences to the fiction page. Working as a PI alongside her lawman/sheriff/private investigator husband, she spent many years teaching by day and 'snooping' by night.

Tapping into her real-world experiences, she writes what she likes to read—faith-based stories, steeped in the mysteries of life's relationships. She is author of the Hamilton Harbor Legacy romance series: *And Then Blooms Love*, *Stumbling Upon Romance*, and *Designed for Love;* and the Seasons of Mystery series: *Autumn Vindication*, *Winter Deception*, *Spring Betrayal*, and *Summer Cover-Up*. She contributed to two novella collections produced by Elk

Lake Publishing, Inc.: *Christmas from the Heart* and *Where Blooms Love.*

Her writing journey began in a small town in central Florida where Spanish moss dressed up the oak trees, orange blossoms scented the air, and thoroughbred racehorse owners dreamed of the Triple Crown. For fun, she wrote storylines that played out like movies in her head. She enjoyed reading Nancy Drew, Hardy Boys, and Alfred Hitchcock stories. So, when given creative writing assignments in school, she loved writing adventures with an unexpected twist at the end.

After declaring her ambition "to do something new and exciting" in her high school yearbook, she left home to attend the University of Florida, thinking she might be an English teacher. But her major changed to pharmacy, which quickly changed to journalism, then fashion design. She transferred to Florida State University where she wound up earning her B.S. and M.S. degrees in home economics education.

Life became a swirl of teaching, marriage, staying home to raise two children, volunteering, returning to the classroom, guidance counseling and honing private investigations skills. Writing during that time centered on lesson plans and PI case reports.

But in 2011, she discovered a Christian writers conference. Meeting with real writers and authors was a thrill. Since then, she has attended several conferences and writing retreats and is a member of Susie May Warren's My Book Therapy, American Christian Fiction Writers, and the Christian Authors Network. She enjoys meeting and encouraging other Christian writers, whether in person, virtually, or through social media.

She resides in north Florida with her schnauzer Gibbs where she enjoys hot mochas, old movies, and dreaming up story plots.

Returning to her love of writing as a youngster, she has come full circle in fulfilling her ambition to do something new and exciting. She believes the scripture in Job best sums up her call to write:

"For I am full of words, and the spirit within me compels me ..."—Job 32:18 (NIV)

You can connect with her at:

- Website http://www.sallyjopitts.com

- Facebook, Author https://www.facebook.com/sallyjopitts

- Twitter https://twitter.com/SallyJoPitts

- Pinterest https://www.pinterest.com/sallyjpitts/

- Amazon Author https://www.amazon.com/author/sallyjopitts

- Instagram https://www.instagram.com/sallyjopitts/

- Sally Jo Pitts' Readers Group https://www.facebook.com/groups/268471081560375

- Bookbub https://www.bookbub.com/profile/sally-jo-pitts?list=author_books

- Goodreads https://www.goodreads.com/author/show/18207570.Sally_Jo_Pitts

OTHER BOOKS BY SALLY JO PITTS

Hamilton Harbor Legacy Series

Winter Solstice Bride
And Then Blooms Love
Stumbling Upon Romance
Designed for Love
The Lost Box: A Hamilton Harbor Christmas

Anthologies

Christmas From the Heart: A Collection of Christian
Romances
Where Blooms Love